Tate pau⟨barcode: S0-BBO-341⟩ walked back up the stairs and wagged a finger in Lily's face.

He'd intended to say something clever, something witty and smart, but when he saw her standing there with that relaxed, happy smile on her face and those deep blue eyes shining behind the lenses of those cute round glasses, every word, every thought went right out of his head except one. He swept his arm around her, folding her close with the crook of his arm. Sliding his free hand over her shoulder blade, he tilted his head and kissed her. This was no accidental kiss.

This was about the woman who made him smile.

Books by Arlene James

ARLENE JAMES

says, "Camp meetings, mission work and church attendance permeate my Oklahoma childhood memories. It was a golden time, which sustains me yet. However, only as a young widowed mother did I truly begin growing in my personal relationship with the Lord. Through adversity He has blessed me in countless ways, one of which is a second marriage so loving and romantic it still feels like courtship!"

After thirty-three years in Texas, Arlene James now resides in Bella Vista, Arkansas, with her beloved husband. Even after seventy-five novels, her need to write is greater than ever, a fact that frankly amazes her, as she's been at it since the eighth grade. She loves to hear from readers, and can be reached via her website, www.arlenejames.com.

Love in Bloom
Arlene James

HARLEQUIN® LOVE INSPIRED®

Special thanks and acknowledgment to Arlene James
for her contribution to
The Heart of Main Street continuity.

Recycling programs
for this product may
not exist in your area.

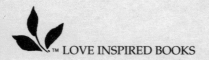

™ LOVE INSPIRED BOOKS

ISBN-13: 978-0-373-81702-3

LOVE IN BLOOM

Copyright © 2013 by Harlequin Books S.A.

www.LoveInspiredBooks.com

Printed in U.S.A.

"For I know the plans I have for you," declares the Lord, "plans to prosper you and not to harm you, plans to give you hope and a future."
—*Jeremiah* 29:11

I dedicate this book to my hometown of Comanche, Oklahoma, where good people still do good things for one another every day and faith is still a way of life.

Prologue

Placing a folder on her desk, Coraline Connolly looked around at the faces of those she had summoned to her office. Tate Bronson shifted his weight from one foot to the other, feeling much like the boy he had once been, waiting for the ax to fall here in the office of the principal of the school. This time, however, he did not fear that he had been caught pulling pranks on his classmates or carving his and Eve's initials into the memorial tree at the corner of Bronson Avenue and School Drive. This time his concerns were not anything as sweetly trivial as losing his privileges at recess or writing extra essays. All here knew that the town they loved teetered on the very edge of disaster.

The problems had begun the moment that Randall Manufacturing had closed its doors, throwing seventy percent of the community's employees out of work. Overnight, Bygones had gone from being one of the most successful small towns in Kansas to a community in decline.

Oh, the townsfolk were still friendly and salt-of-the-earth, willing to give the shirts off their backs to friends and neighbors in need. The original Bronson Homestead, now home to the public library, a spacious park with a sizable playground, charming gazebo and shady pond, still welcomed visitors with its sylvan peace. The lazy streets where children played and houses stood in safety with doors unlocked were still realities of the friendly ambience of the small town. Sadly, however, what they had once taken for granted in Bygones was no longer secure.

In the months since the closing of Randall Manufacturing, other businesses had shuttered. Homes had been abandoned and repossessed as people moved out in search of work. Mayor Langston had even been forced to shut down the butcher department in his grocery store. With revenues dropping like a lead weight in a pail of water, the city had been forced to lay off personnel and scale back services. When the bank branch had closed, the whole town had known that it was in real trouble. Tate couldn't help wondering if Robert Randall truly realized what he'd done to this community when he'd shuttered his aerospace manufacturing plant.

Miss Coraline, who at sixty had been a fixture at the school for over thirty years, had been deeply disappointed because the annual alumni banquet had been called off due to a lack of funds. Canceling the alumni banquet was the least of the problems for the school, however. Tate very much feared that Coraline had gathered this diverse group today—arguably now Bygones' most influential citizens—to announce that the school would close entirely, with the county absorbing its students.

As if reading his thoughts, Coraline stood behind her desk and pulled herself up to her full height, which must have been all of an inch over five feet, and said, "You must be wondering why I've called you all here."

Mayor Langston, seated next to old Miss Mars, stacked his hands atop the curved head of his cane and replied, "I hope for good news, but I confess that I expect the opposite."

"We've had nothing but bad news for months now," Joe Sheridan, the chief of police and an ex-marine, pointed out with a sigh.

"We mustn't lose hope," Dale Eversleigh, the colorful, rotund, fortyish town undertaker counseled.

"Easy for you to say," muttered Elwood Dill, proprietor of The Everything, the town's most successful retail business. "Your services never go out of demand. I have people buying gasoline one gallon at a time now and eating candy bars for dinner."

Miss Ann Mars tilted back her snowy head and smiled at the fifty-something, long-haired, tattooed, self-proclaimed "flower child."

"You're giving away as many gallons of gasoline

and hamburgers as you sell, Elwood, and don't you deny it."

Elwood shrugged, and Tate smiled to himself. Elwood and his wife might be a bit unconventional, but like almost everyone else around Bygones, they were good people. The question was if the town founded by Tate's great-great-grandfather, Paul Bronson, and his brother, Saul, would still be around for these good people or if it would become another of the many ghost towns littering the Kansas plains. Tate looked to Coraline Connolly, who had always been a voice of steady reason in the community.

"Don't keep us in suspense, ma'am. Why are we here?"

"Answered prayer, Tate," she announced, smiling as she held up a large empty envelope stamped as Certified Mail. "I do believe it's answered prayer." She flipped open the folder on her desk and spread out its contents. "I received this two days ago, and it's taken me a while to fully understand all of the ramifications. I want you all to know that I consulted an attorney about this before I called you here."

The mayor picked up one of the papers and began to read, while Miss Mars did the same with another. Miss Mars reported first.

"A holding company is purchasing the entire south side of Main Street!"

"All those empty stores that are now in receivership?" Eversleigh queried, obviously perplexed.

"And updating them!" Miss Mars went on, continuing to read.

"Whatever for?" Joe Sheridan asked.

"New businesses," Mayor Langston answered, a note of awe in his tone. "In the very heart of Main Street."

"What new businesses?" Elwood Dill scoffed.

"The new businesses we choose to bring in," Coraline said, pressing her hands flat upon the desk, "with the grants funded by an anonymous benefactor."

"I don't believe this," Dale Eversleigh exclaimed, all but snatching the paper from Mayor Langston's hands.

Langston fell back in his chair. "If we can save Main Street, we can save the town."

"Are you actually saying," Joe demanded, seeking clarification, "that this is what we've been praying for?"

They had been praying, Tate knew. They'd held many a prayer meeting at the Bygones Community Church these past months. Tate had attended none of them, but he knew well what had been said. He knew, too, that God often failed to hear or answer prayer.

"Hold on, now," he said, determined to be the voice of reason. "Who is this benefactor?"

Coraline shook her head. "I don't know. Whoever it is insists on anonymity."

"But why do this for Bygones?"

"I can't answer that, either, but it must be some-one with a connection to the town. We can't be the only ones who love this place. I keep thinking that it must be a former student. Otherwise why send all this to me? All I know for sure, though, is what's in these papers."

Tate thought about that. The school was small. This two-story redbrick building housed all twelve grades and kindergarten, but hundreds of students had passed through its hallowed halls in the time Miss Coraline had been here. Most had now moved on.

"How do we know it's legitimate?"

"An account has been set up," Eversleigh re-ported, looking up from the papers, "and there's an email address for consultation. All we have to do is put together a committee, set parameters for the grants, take applications, make our choices and apprise our benefactor of them. The monies will then be released to the recipients."

"The holding company will take care of pre-paring the shops to accommodate the needs of the businesses that we choose," Miss Mars reported.

"What have we got to lose?" Chief Sheridan asked excitedly.

"Exactly my opinion," the mayor agreed, sitting up straight, "and it seems to me that the first order of business is to form that committee. Coraline, since this comes to us through you, I'd say that chore falls in your lap."

"Which is why I've asked you all here," she told them. "I've given this a lot of thought and a lot of prayer, and as far as I'm concerned, *you* are the committee. If you're all willing, that is."

They looked at one another, nodding.

"I think you mean, *we* are the committee, don't you?" Tate said to Coraline. She smiled, a look of hope on her face.

"The Save Our Streets Committee," Elwood quipped with a grin. "SOS for short. Sounds appropriate, don't you think?"

"Sounds hopeful to me," Miss Mars all but sang.

"It's about time something did," Joe Sheridan said, gulping audibly.

"So long as it works," Dale Eversleigh intoned.

"Please, God," Coraline breathed.

"Speaking of work," Mayor Langston said, reaching for a pen from the utensil cup on Coraline's desk, "I have some ideas about those grant parameters…"

Tate hung back as the others bent over the principal's desk, eagerly following the mayor's line of thought as he sketched it out with notes. Though he was by far the youngest member of this ad hoc committee, his thoughts had gone back in time.

No one could have asked for a better place to grow up than Bygones, Kansas. No one could ask for a better place to raise their daughter. No one grieved the calamities that had befallen their hometown or feared its demise more than Tate. But anonymous benefactors and mysterious holding companies were almost as difficult for Tate to accept as a God who heard and answered the desperate prayers of His children. For no one knew better than Tate how little God truly cared.

Still, as an heir of the founding family—which was no doubt why Miss Coraline had chosen him for the SOS Committee—Tate would do all that he could to save the town. Never mind that he didn't live within its city limits. A ranching and farming family, the Bronsons lived on a large acreage outside of town, but their forebears had platted the city's streets, established its institutions, sent their children to its school, shopped in its stores, called its citizens their friends and neighbors—and buried their dead in its cemetery. This was his town, and like everyone else around here, he'd lost enough already. So, he made up his mind.

Anonymous benefactor or no anonymous benefactor, Bygones, Kansas, wasn't going down without a fight. That meant Tate Bronson would do everything in his power to make this crazy scheme work. The others could pray all they wanted, but Tate would keep a clear head and make wise choices. They'd bring new blood and new businesses to town, and with them would come hope and, maybe, just maybe, new life.

Chapter One

The pavement outside the Kansas City Airport radiated heat even though the sun had already sunk below the horizon. Tate held his nearly eight-year-old daughter's hand a little tighter and resisted the urge to shake out his long legs and hurry along as they crossed the traffic lane to the sidewalk. He pushed back the brim of his straw cowboy hat and squinted against the dying sunshine to read the signs hanging overhead.

"That's it down there," he said, pointing. "Baggage Claim A."

They hurried in that direction, Isabella skipping ahead. The hem was coming down on the back side of her favorite purple T-shirt. He'd have to ask his mom to buy her a new one to match the embroidery on her favorite pair of jeans. Meanwhile Ms. Lily Farnsworth would just have to excuse his daughter's attire, as well as his lateness. And the heat.

Lifting his hat, he mopped his forehead with his

shirtsleeve. The first day of July had dawned hot and clear. He hoped that Ms. Farnsworth, being from Boston, was prepared for what she would find here in Kansas.

Lily Farnsworth was the last of six new business owners to arrive, each selected by the Save Our Streets Committee, dubbed the SOS, of the town of Bygones. As a member of the committee, Tate had been asked to meet her at the airport in Kansas City, transport her to Bygones and act as her official host and contact. With the Grand Opening just a week away, most of the shop owners had been at work preparing their stores for some time already, but Ms. Farnsworth had delayed until after her sister's wedding, assuring the committee that a florist's shop required less preparation than some retail businesses. Tate hoped she was right.

He still wasn't convinced that this scheme, financed by a mysterious, anonymous donor, would work. But if something didn't revive the financial fortunes of Bygones—and soon—their small town would become just another ghost town on the north central plains. Tate thought of the school where he had met his late wife and of the cemetery where he had buried her nearly eight years ago, and he ached to think of those places abandoned and forgotten, so he would do what he could to revive the community.

Isabella stopped before the automatic doors and waited for him to catch up. He did so quickly, and they entered the cool building together. A pair of gleaming luggage carousels occupied the open space, both vacant. A few people milled about. Some wore uniforms of one sort or another; most just seemed to be waiting. One, a tall, slender, pretty woman with long blond hair and round tortoiseshell glasses, perched atop a veritable mountain of luggage. She wore black ballet slippers and white knit leggings beneath a gossamery blue dress with fluttery sleeves and hems. Her very long hair parted in the middle and waved about her face and shoulders. As he watched, she gathered that pale gold hair in slim-fingered hands with tiny knuckles, twisted it into a long rope and pulled it over one shoulder. Her gaze touched his then skittered away. He felt the insane urge to look closer, behind the lenses of those glasses that gave her a calm, intelligent air, but of course, he would not.

For one thing, Tate Bronson did not interest himself in attractive women. For another, that could not be Lily Farnsworth. Lily Farnsworth was a florist from Boston, not a blonde—he glanced back at the woman seated on the baggage—with the air of a ballet dancer and librarian combined. He turned away, the better to resist the urge to stare, and scanned the building for anyone who might be his florist. Maybe he should have made a sign; but then, he wasn't a limo driver. He was a rancher and farmer trying to help keep his town from dying a slow, certain death. He'd have felt like an idiot standing there with a hand-lettered sign.

One by one the possibilities faded away, greeted by others or disappearing on their own. Finally Isabella gave him that look that said *Dad, you're being a goof again.* She slipped her little hand into his, and he sighed inwardly. Of course the pretty blonde was not a ballet dancer or librarian at all. And she'd packed up half of Boston to bring with her. Even with the long-bed pickup truck out there in the parking lot, a good number of those suitcases and boxes would have to go into the backseat with Isabella. So, an idiot with or without the sign. Great. Turning, he walked the few yards to the luggage mountain and swept off his straw cowboy hat.

"Are you Lily Farnsworth by any chance?"

A slender forefinger with a blunt tip and a knuckle so delicate it seemed made of paste came up to push those round glasses more firmly onto a nose as straight and fine as a blade. She nodded just once and rose, brushing at her filmy skirt, a clear blue like the darkly fringed eyes behind the lenses of her glasses. Her ivory-pink skin, completely devoid of cosmetics, showed a sprinkling of freckles across cheeks that bunched into pale apples when she smiled—and what a smile it was. She had perfect lips, wide and mobile, not too thin and not too thick, a luscious natural dusty pink against blindingly white, even teeth. A square-tipped chin on an oval face completed the picture.

"I'm Lily," she said in a voice as gossamery as her skirts. "You must be Tate Bronson. What a pleasure it is to meet you. I was expecting a grizzled old rancher, not a handsome, young…well…"

She bowed her head, her blond hair flowing forward to hide her reddening face. Tate frowned, not at all liking the way his heart sped up. Yep, no sign needed. He was perfectly capable of behaving like an idiot without any props.

Looking down at her comfortable flat slippers, Lily willed away the color swamping her face. Honestly, she'd gotten over this awkwardness long ago. Hadn't she? If only she hadn't been staring at him all this time, she'd have had more control of her tongue. That and fatigue had gotten the better of her. To get the best price, she'd flown from Boston to Atlanta to Kansas City, which had made for a long day. Suddenly she wished she'd taken more pains with her appearance, but why bother when she was so tall and thin and wore glasses? Men generally failed to notice her at all, and when they did, they treated her like their sisters or their maiden aunts. This one would barely even look at her. No doubt his wife was the next thing to a fashion model. A man as attractive as him would naturally marry a woman like that.

Tall and muscular, with thick, dark brown hair worn so short that the circular cowlicks at his crown and the center of his forehead were clearly visible, he had smooth features and warm brown eyes in a squarish face marked by dimples even when he wasn't smiling. Given the thickness of his hair, his brows seemed surprisingly slender, and if he had a fault then it was the thinness of his lips. Or was that simply his frown? The little redheaded imp with him seemed undeterred by his scowl. She skipped forward and put out a chubby hand.

"Hi! I'm Isabella. I'm seven, almost eight. How old are you?"

"Isabella," Tate Bronson scolded. "You don't ask a lady her age."

"Why not? I'm a lady, and I told her mine."

"I'm sorry," Bronson apologized, his frown softening. He really was quite attractive, especially when he wasn't frowning. "My daughter is looking forward to her birthday later this month, but that's no excuse for her being rude."

"That's all right," Lily said with a smile. Switching her gaze to the girl, Lily bent forward. "It's a pleasure to meet you, Isabella." Dropping her voice to a stage whisper, she confessed, "I turned twenty-seven on May Day."

Isabella cut her blue-eyed glance up at her father, drawling, "Twenty-seven's good. Daddy's twenty-seven. His birthday's in September. Then he'll be twenty-eight."

Lily felt a jolt of surprise. Twenty-eight with an eight-year-old. That made him a very young father.

Tate made an impatient sound and said, "Can we get going, please? We have a long drive ahead of us."

"Oh, of course," Lily said apologetically, gathering her voluminous handbag and backpack. She slung one over each shoulder, stacked two of the smaller boxes atop one of the larger wheeled bags and prepared to haul out the lot.

"Wait," Tate said. "Let's do this with some organization."

Feeling chastised, Lily ducked her head, her long hair sliding forward. "Okay. Uh, what would you suggest?"

He pulled up the handle on one of the smaller wheeled bags and handed it to Isabella, then tossed a box onto his shoulder and snagged the handle of the larger bag from Lily, saying, "Wait here with the rest. We'll take out these and be back."

Lily bit back a protest. Those were vases and other glass items balanced on his shoulder, going-away gifts from her friends in Boston, things to help her get started in Bygones. Her former employer and coworkers knew how carefully she had budgeted to make this plan feasible, even selling her beloved car to raise the necessary funds to match the grant and choosing a shop with living quarters above it to cut expenses. She had packed those particular items carefully for shipping and sent them ahead of her to be collected when she arrived at the airport; she supposed they would survive Tate Bronson, so she bit her lip and watched him walk away without saying a word. His daughter followed him, her long red curls bouncing merrily. Lily noticed idly that the hem of the child's purple T-shirt had come down, but her mind was too preoccupied with her new venture to assign any significance to that fact.

While helping her sister pick out flowers for her upcoming wedding, the florist, a former employer of Lily's, had surreptitiously handed her a newspaper article about a place in Kansas taking applications for matching grants for businesses willing to locate in the small town of Bygones. The applicants had to submit a business plan, deposit funds equal to the amount of the requested grant, agree to hire locals and complete a minimum two-year residency. Failure to maintain the required residency and keep the business in operation would constitute a default, in which case, the grant would have to be repaid within five years. Knowing that Lily hated what she was currently doing for a living and much preferred the work that she'd done while attending college and graduate school—namely, floral design—this friend and former employer had encouraged Lily to apply for one of the grants.

Lily had considered it answered prayer when she had been chosen as one of the grant recipients, but she hadn't told her family of her plans until the last moment. They had not taken it well. She couldn't blame them.

It was one thing to find a nail in one's soup; it was another when that nail swam to the top of the bowl and climbed out. Lily was now the only florist in a family of lawyers. Oh, she had the degree and the law license, but she was not, strictly speaking, a lawyer, at least not anymore. Now she was a florist, which meant that it was do-or-die for her here in Kansas.

Everything depended on making this work. Lily had staked everything on this scheme. Should she fail in Bygones, she would be buried in debt, and returning to her former occupation would be her only alternative, even if she wasn't very good at it. Worse, it would mean returning home to the bosom of her family, and that she did not want under any circumstances but especially not in defeat. If she was to be the maiden aunt to her sister's children, she would be so at a distance with a successful business to occupy her time and mind. She would not hang around Boston, pretending she wasn't miserable and envious, while her sister and new brother-in-law started their family, something they were eager to do.

No, it was bad enough that her sister had married the man whom Lily had wanted for herself. Lily didn't have to stick around and watch them have babies, not when she so wanted babies, too. If she couldn't have a family of her own, Lily would do whatever it took to build a successful business in Bygones. That included, she reminded herself as Tate Bronson and his adorable daughter moved toward her once more, those things that went against her nature, such as speaking up. So, as he bent to take up another of her boxes, she found her voice.

"Uh, if you…if you could be careful."

He gave her such a look, as if she were an inanimate object suddenly come to life, but he took great care stacking the boxes and hoisting them onto his shoulders. He then turned and walked away without a word. Isabella took up her backpack, chattering.

"I'll have to sit in the corner, but it's okay. I don't mind. Daddy shoulda left the bags of feed at home. He didn't figure you'd have so much stuff."

"I see," Lily muttered. She quickly took the backpack from Isabella and shouldered it once more, then pulled up the handle on one of the medium bags. "Think you can handle that?"

"Uh-huh."

Using both hands, Isabella began pulling the bag toward the door. Lily stacked the remaining two boxes atop the remaining suitcase and, also using both hands, began backing toward the door. They made the sidewalk before Tate returned to scoop up boxes and bags.

"Come on."

Lily tried to explain herself as they crossed the street and trailed across the parking lot. "I, um, looked into standard shipping, but it was cheaper to check some things as luggage and send the rest as air freight, and this way I have it all on hand when I arrive. I—I'm sorry I didn't think to warn anyone that I would have extra luggage."

He shrugged. "Part of my responsibilities."

"Do you mind if I ask what your responsibilities are, I mean, so far as I'm concerned?"

"Get you there. Make sure you get set up in time for the Grand Opening."

"Very good. I appreciate that."

He seemed to thaw a bit then. "I'm your official contact with the committee and your host, at least through the Grand Opening reception."

"Oh. All right. That's nice. Thank you."

"No problem. When you're ready to hire help, I'll have a list of names for you, too."

"Ah. That will be useful."

"When do you think you'll be ready to hire someone, by the way?"

"Um, soon after the Grand Opening, I should think."

"I see."

"That is, if it's successful."

"The town's done its part," he told her.

"That's good to know. What can you tell me about the town? I mean, beyond the statistics."

He seemed to consider for a moment before saying, "Nothing much to tell." Lily's spirits sagged. She was tired and uncertain and hoping for a warm welcome, not this terse, tepid greeting. "You'll see soon enough," he added, stopping next to a dirty white double-cab pickup truck. He placed one of the boxes in the bed of the truck. Lily took a deep breath.

"Um, do you…do you think we could put those boxes inside?"

He turned a surprised look on her. "You want those particular boxes inside, not the suitcases?"

"What's in the boxes is more valuable," she said, pushing up her glasses.

He lifted his eyebrows. "Okay. If that's the way you want it."

"Yes, thank you," she replied softly.

He reached into his pocket and an electronic beep sounded. He opened the back door of the cab and wrestled the big suitcase to the ground then transferred boxes to the inside. It took some shifting around, but they finally got everything loaded. As soon as they were all belted into their seats, Tate behind the wheel, Lily on the front passenger side and Isabella in a booster seat behind Lily in the back, Isabella spoke up.

"Daddy got on the SOS 'cause we're Bronsons."

"SOS?"

"It's short for Save Our Streets," he explained, starting the engine. "That's the name of the committee that chose the businesses that got the grants."

"Yes, I remember reading that in the paperwork, but what does being Bronsons have to do with it?"

"Bronsons founded the town," he answered brusquely.

"They were brothers," Isabella volunteered, "and one of 'em runned off with the other one's sweetheart, so they hated each other."

"Oh, dear," Lily murmured.

"They got over it," Tate stated matter-of-factly, and that was that.

Lily sighed mentally. She'd imagined a sweet little town, pulling together to do something grand, not feuding founders and "nothing much to tell."

Suddenly Isabella piped up from the backseat again. "Are you married?"

"What? Uh. No."

"Daddy's not married, either."

So, no fashion model wife then. That explained the falling-down hem on Isabella's T-shirt. No conscientious mother would let such a pretty little girl go out with the hem coming down on her T-shirt, or so Lily imagined. A single father, now, he probably wouldn't even notice such a thing. While Lily wondered about Isabella's mother, Isabella wondered about other things, and she wasn't the least bit shy in letting Lily know.

"Have you got a boyfriend?"

"Isabella!" Tate barked.

Lily cringed. "No, I don't have a boyfriend, either."

"How come?"

"Well, I—I just…" Lily felt her face heat.

"Don't you want to get married and have children?"

My, what a direct child. "Y-yes. Very much."

"Do you like babies? I like babies."

"I love babies."

"My friend Bonnie has a baby sister. I want a baby sister."

Lily shot a glance at Tate Bronson, who was not married. Perhaps he and Isabella's mother were divorced, and his ex-wife had remarried, and Isabella was hoping for a baby sister from that quarter. If so, that might explain the granitelike tightness of Tate's profile just then.

"Isabella, that's enough!" Tate ordered. "You pipe down now."

"Okay, Daddy."

"I mean it. Not another word."

"Yes, sir."

Lily sank down in her seat, feeling the undercurrents swirl around her. She didn't know Tate Bronson's story, but she knew her own.

Didn't she want to get married and have children? Oh, yes. Very much. But that wasn't likely when she didn't even have a boyfriend, when she hadn't *ever* had a boyfriend. And why was that? Wasn't it obvious? Painfully obvious, she imagined, at least to Tate. Maybe not to his precocious daughter.

She just wasn't the sort men noticed or in which they developed interest. She'd had ample proof of that already. She didn't need any more, not from Tate Bronson or anyone else.

Lily turned her unseeing gaze out the quickly darkening window and prayed that she hadn't made a horrible mistake in coming to Kansas.

Chapter Two

Her first sight of Bygones was not encouraging. Once they had gotten beyond the confines of the city, the landscape had seemed pleasantly green with rolling hills and lots of trees. About an hour out, however, that had gradually given way to flat golden plains and mere lines of trees following creeks and streams. By the time they reached the outskirts of Bygones, everything seemed dusty and barren in the moonlight. Lily pointed at a tall, ghostly shape rising sharply out of the dark.

"What is that?"

"Grain elevator," came the terse reply.

They passed a scattering of low buildings next to the tall ones, and a little farther down the road they came to a block of small clapboard houses surrounded by too many vehicles and too little fencing. A few trees spread stunted branches and dark shadows. A dog ran to the edge of the road and barked madly as they passed. Tate paid it no mind, the

truck speeding on. It slowed a few moments later
as more substantial homes and buildings came into
view. They passed the back of a small post office
and a drive-through drop-off box. A few seconds
later the truck turned right onto Main Street.

Lily caught her breath. This was more like it.
Old-fashioned wrought-iron lampposts, topped now
with pairs of American flags; illuminated matching
benches placed strategically along the wide sidewalk. Ornamental evergreens in enormous terra-
cotta pots complemented the brick pavement of the
wide street and sprouted tiny flags amongst their
needles. The buildings on both sides of the street
had been painted a creamy yellow-tan and fronted
with colorful awnings, now draped with patriotic
bunting. The woodwork around the recessed doors
and the large display windows had been painted to
complement the awning colors. The buildings were
old, perhaps from the 1930s, but looked to be in excellent condition.

On the south side of the street, every shop window bore a banner that read, "Welcome!"

Below that another sign read, "Happy Independence Day!"

Lily's gaze sought out the spring-green awning
with the heart-shaped scarlet lily gracefully arc-
ing across it. The words below it in flowing script
read, "Love in Bloom." A scarlet heart dotted the *i*.
Lily laughed in delight. It looked exactly as she had
designed it, exactly as she had submitted it.

Tate glanced at her, asking, "So far so good?"

"It's exactly what I hoped it would look like."

He nodded. "Everyone says the contractors and consultants have done excellent work."

Tate traveled on past the shop to the four-way stop at the intersection of Main and Bronson. Since hers was the second shop from the corner, it wasn't far. He didn't bother to actually stop, simply slowed and hooked a U-turn in the wide intersection.

"Is that legal?"

He shrugged. "It's late. No other traffic. I wouldn't try it in the daytime, though."

"Since I don't have a vehicle, I don't expect it'll be a problem."

Shaking his head, he said, "I can't help wondering how you figure on getting around out here without your own transportation."

"Oh, I'm going to live in the apartment above the shop."

"Yeah, I know, but—"

"I'm told there's a grocery up the street."

"Sure. It'll do if you're not too picky."

"And there's a doctor a couple blocks over."

"Tuesdays and Thursdays only."

He pulled the truck over to the curb in front of the shop and killed the engine but made no move to get out.

"What about restaurants?" Lily asked.

"Uh, well, there's the grill at The Everything for

lunch and dinner. That's like half a block behind you, but the menu's pretty limited."

"Hmm."

"I'm not quite sure what you can get at the Cozy Cup Café after it opens, not much more than some fancy coffee and snacks, if I remember the prospectus correctly." He glanced at the shop on the corner next door, adding, "The bakery will open soon, too. That ought to get you breakfast and some yummy desserts. That's about it, though."

"Okay. Well, I probably ought to be eating in more often anyway."

"That's what we do."

She thought for a moment of all the lovely dinners out that she'd enjoyed in Boston, of the oyster bars and bistros, the pizzerias and one-of-a-kind "fusion" restaurants, the Back Bay seafood and Beacon Hill steaks. She thought of friends and family left behind, and her spirits wavered, but then she thought of new friends to be made and a business of her own, a new life in a new place. Her chin rose in determination.

A sound came from the backseat of the truck, the kind a sleeping child makes when perfectly at ease and content. Little Isabella Bronson of the flaming red hair and bright blue eyes slept peacefully behind them in her father's pickup truck, apparently as content as if she were at home in her own bed. Smiling, Lily looked up at that awning and the front of the shop. Her gaze rose to the darkened windows above the awning. Her apartment. Her own shop and home. It was a far cry from Boston, but it was hers, her chance to do something real, something besides practice law and be miserable. This was her chance to break the mold, to prove herself, to be someone she liked and admired, not just a failed Farnsworth clone, yearning for what could not be.

Dorothy, she thought flippantly, *we* are *in Kansas!*

And maybe this wasn't a mistake. Maybe, for once, she'd done the right thing.

Oh, Lord, she silently prayed for the thousandth time since she'd read that article and filled out the application, *please help me do the right things. For once in my life, please help me get it right.*

Glancing into the backseat, Tate saw that Isabella still slept soundly. She'd dropped off soon after they'd left the environs of Kansas City, which was no surprise considering that the hour had been well past her normal bedtime. He should have left her with his parents instead of dragging her along on this trip, but that would have meant allowing her to sleep over, and he hated when she did that. Even after all these years he couldn't get used to sleeping out at his place alone. When he'd first brought her home from the hospital, a new father and a widower, he'd wondered if he'd ever sleep again. But they'd found their way together, and now he couldn't seem to manage without her even for a single night. His mother said that he sometimes held on to Isabella too tightly, but he didn't know how else to hold her.

Lily Farnsworth got out of the truck and all but skipped across the sidewalk to the door of her shop and back again, her excitement palpable. Tate took the keys from the pocket of his jeans and tossed them to her. Catching them easily, she graced him with a smile before spinning away again. He watched her fit the key into the lock and turn it. The door swung wide. Lily reached inside and flipped on the lights; then she glided over the threshold into the bare space filled only with two small glass-fronted humidifiers to display the flowers, several large flat boxes, a small unpainted waist-high counter and a steel worktable half-hidden behind a wall at the back of the room.

She poked around for a bit while Tate unloaded suitcases from the bed of the truck and hauled them onto the sidewalk. Emerging from the building a few minutes later, she pronounced the place, "Perfect."

"Looks like it needs some work to me," Tate teased, unable to resist her enthusiasm.

Her smile instantly dissolved. "What I mean is, it's perfect for my purposes."

He felt like a heel. Irritated with himself, he waved a hand at the door beside the shop, the one between her business and the bookstore next door.

"If you'll open that door, I'll carry these up to your apartment."

"Oh, most of those don't go to the apartment," she said, pointing into the shop. "They go in here."

Tate reached up to push back the brim of his hat, realized he'd left it in the truck and parked his hands at his waist. "What about the boxes?"

"Most of those go into the shop, too."

"Didn't you bring anything to set up housekeeping?"

"A few things. It's mostly shop supplies, though. You know, vases, foam, tubes, frogs, wires, tape, cones, hooks, hangers, ribbon, pins, charms, feathers, silk flowers…"

"Frogs?"

"Uh, to hold pins. They're not real frogs." She seemed embarrassed. "They don't even look like real frogs." She shrugged and bowed her head. "That's just what we call them."

Tate swallowed a chuckle and shifted his weight from one booted foot to another, finding her shyness kind of cute. "I figured you'd order supplies."

"Well, yes, I have ordered some things, but why order what I already have? Especially when I didn't have to pay for these things. They were gifts from my former employer and coworkers at the flower shop in Boston. Going-away gifts. 'Success gifts,' they called them."

The lady knew how to pinch a penny. "Okay, I get it now. So which of these suitcases goes upstairs?"

"Just the big one."

"All right. Let's get these others inside, then I'll take that one upstairs."

They rolled the other suitcases into the shop. Lily positioned them behind the work area wall while Tate went out to remove the boxes from the backseat of the truck. Isabella woke as he worked, rubbed her eyes with both fists and pronounced herself in need of a potty.

"Go inside there," Tate instructed. "There's a bathroom in back." He heard her asking Lily, and the two of them went off to find "the ladies' room," as Lily called it. Tate knew that it was a modest little necessary tucked into a corner.

"That's going to need some attention," Lily muttered upon their return.

By that he assumed she meant decoration, which was her department. He nodded to the boxes. "Any of these go upstairs?"

She pointed out only two of the smaller ones.

"All right. Then if you'll each tote one, I'll take the big suitcase, and we'll go up."

Nodding, Lily took the larger of the two boxes and stood by the door while Isabella easily carried her box and her father followed. Lily glanced around once more, shut off the lights and stepped outside to close the door and lock up before moving to the door that led to the apartment upstairs. Lily began searching for the appropriate key.

"Uh, I'm pretty sure that door's not locked," Tate told her.

She pushed her glasses up on her nose and looked at him as if he'd suddenly grown a second head. "What do you mean?"

"Well, the workmen were coming and going, and no one could say exactly when the bed you ordered would be delivered. It was just easier to leave it open."

Her jaw dropped. "Even after the bed came?"

"Sure. I didn't see the point in…" She found the light switch and flipped it on, illuminating the narrow, enclosed staircase. "Why lock the door on an empty apartment?" he asked as she slipped inside and started climbing the stairs. Tate stepped up and blocked the door open with his shoulder, calling after her, "No one locks their doors around here, not to their houses." She ignored him and kept climbing.

Tate indicated with a nod that Isabella should go next. Shrugging, she started up after Lily, who quickly reached the small landing at the top and let herself into the apartment. A light came on in the small foyer. Isabella followed. Tate came last into the dark but spacious living and dining area.

"What is this place?" Isabella asked.

"This is my home," Lily told her, coming out of the dark hallway behind her. Lily quickly moved into the small kitchen and switched on a light there. "Not many overhead lights in here. I'll need to buy some lamps."

"You're going to live in town?" Isabella asked doubtfully.

"Right above my shop," Lily confirmed, "in the very heart of Main Street."

"We live in the country. Right, Dad?"

"Yep."

"On the ranch. Right, Dad?"

"Right."

"Grandpa, though, he calls it the farm. Don't he, Daddy?"

"That's because he's in charge of the farming end of things."

"And Daddy, he does the horses and the cows and all the animal stuff. And he helps with the farm, too, and sometimes the tractor stuff. And he and Grandpa do the oil lease stuff together."

"You talk too much," he told her, nudging her with the suitcase. He looked to Lily and asked, "So where do you want these?"

She took the box from Isabella, saying, "I'll put this in the bathroom. You can just leave that there, though."

Tate nodded. "If you didn't notice, there's a coat closet here."

"That's convenient."

"And there's a walk-in closet in the front bedroom. I had them set up the bed in there. The back room is really small, but you could put a twin bed in there for company."

She looked around the empty living area and said, "I think I'll concentrate on a couch first."

Tate chuckled. "Yeah, or a chair at least."

She smiled and nodded. "I understood there was a washer and dryer."

"That closet in the kitchen," he said. "It's one of those stacked jobs with the dryer on top."

"That's fine."

"Okay, well…"

Isabella pointed at the trio of bare windows overlooking the vacant, softly lit street. Tilting her curly head, she asked, "Who's that?"

Tate and Lily both moved toward the window, staring at the wildly waving figure in the window of the building across the street.

"Oh, that," Tate said with a grin. "That's Miss Ann Mars. You know her."

"Sure. Ever'body knows Miss Mars. She's had her shop in Bygones forever."

"I guess you didn't know that she lives downtown above her shop, too."

"This 'N' That," Lily read the sign on the awning across the street. "What sort of shop is it?"

"Um, sundries," Tate answered. "You know, needles and pins, candles, handkerchiefs, coin purses, hand mirrors, little stuff. That's in the front. Out back, now that's—how do I put this?—mostly junk, I guess."

Lily raised her eyebrows. Her glasses slid down her nose, so she pushed them back up. Tate fought the urge to smile for some reason. Clearing his throat, he turned away from the window at the same time Miss Mars did.

"Miss Ann is on the committee," he told Lily, pulling a card from his shirt pocket. "If you need something and you can't reach me, you can always tell Miss Mars." He pressed the card into Lily's hand and started for the door.

"I'll walk you down," Lily said. "I want to take another look at the shop."

Shrugging, he turned a sleepy-eyed Isabella toward the stairs. He ushered his daughter out onto the landing then slipped past her and down a few steps before turning and gathering her into his arms. She laid her precious red head on his shoulders. Laying his cheek against those bright curls, he thought of his late wife, Eve, and the old familiar ache of loss filled him. If their daughter could have known Eve for even a little while, she'd give up her matchmaking ways, but the imp had never known her mother.

After carrying his daughter down the stairs, he nodded at Ann Mars, who scampered across the street in her bedroom slippers and housedress, the coil of her long white hair sliding to and fro atop her head. The tiny, bent old woman had to be eighty if she was a day, and as far as Tate knew, she had never married. If she had family, he was unaware of them. Stepping up onto the curb, she crossed the sidewalk to greet Lily.

Tate made the introduction. "Miss Mars, Lily Farnsworth. Lily, Miss Ann Mars, SOS Committee member and your neighbor."

"So happy to meet you!" Miss Mars exclaimed,

bending far backward to get a good look at the newcomer. "You're aptly named for a florist."

Lily smiled and pushed her glasses up. "I guess I am, at that."

Miss Mars stuck her nose to the window of Lily's shop, asking, "What are in those big boxes in there?"

"Glass shelving."

"You'll have to put it together, I expect," Tate stated, and Lily nodded. "You have the tools for it and everything?"

She blinked behind those round glasses. "Uh, not exactly."

Not exactly. Tate shook his head. He supposed he'd better show up tomorrow morning prepared to get those shelves together for her.

"I have to get my girl home to bed," he said, carrying his daughter to the truck.

Lily called out her thanks as he belted Isabella into her seat. Already thinking about what he would need to bring with him in the morning, he shut the truck door, walked around and got in behind the wheel. He'd be more comfortable about the whole thing if Lily Farnsworth looked less like a fetching, ballet-dancing librarian and more like Miss Ann Mars, but Tate was not one to shirk his responsibilities, no matter how much he might want to.

Looking up from the half-finished shelving unit the next morning, Lily tilted back her head to peer through her glasses and the thick beveled glass insert of her shop door. She'd already hung a little brass bell over the heavy green door, and it tinkled pleasantly, evoking a smile even before she recognized Tate's tall, muscular figure. He carried a heavy, somewhat battered metal toolbox at his side. Pushing back the bill of his faded red cap, he stared down at her, his frown at odds with the dimples in his cheeks.

"How'd you get that together without tools?"

She lifted a screwdriver with one hand and a pair of pliers with the other, wishing she'd worn jeans instead of baggy leggings and a cute top instead of this shapeless, oversize T-shirt. Then again, when was she ever really at her best?

"Miss Ann had a few things out back of her shop. We dug around out there after breakfast, although I have to tell you, I think she knows exactly where to find every item in the place."

"Huh." He set down the heavy toolbox and parked his hands at his belt, brown to match his round-toed boots.

"Where's Isabella?" Lily asked, getting up off the floor and dusting off her behind with both hands, though earlier she'd swept the finely refinished wood floor with a broom that she'd picked up at the This 'N' That.

"With my folks."

"Ah." Not with her mother then.

He glanced around at the spring green walls. The

short wall in the back had been painted a rich scarlet. He pointed at the unpainted counter. "You didn't specify what color you wanted that, so the contractor just left some cans of paint in the back."

"I'm thinking lavender," she told him, "with the logo and name of the store on the front. I can freehand it later."

"Really? You can just grab a paintbrush and do that by hand?" He lifted an eyebrow skeptically. "Okay, if you say so. What about the humidifiers?"

Confused, Lily shook her head. "They don't need painting."

"I mean, have you decided how to fasten them down? State code requires it. Better let me take care of it now. Where do you want them?"

"Hmm, the one in the work area needs to be in the back corner facing this direction." She held up her hands to demonstrate how she wanted it to face, and he went off to take care of it while she continued to work on the shelving.

Fifteen minutes of scraping and drilling later, he was back in the front of the shop and ready to tackle the display unit there.

"Where do you want this one?"

She pointed to the corner. He shoved the humidifier easily into position, but then she changed her mind. For a good half hour after that, he shoved the thing around from one spot to another, finally winding up right back where they'd started.

"I'm sorry. I—I just wasn't certain."

He shrugged, and got out his drill. "Better to be sure."

They worked in relative silence, the buzz of his power drill the only sound. Every once in a while, a vehicle rolled down the street, stopped at the four-way stop sign and went on its way. People walked along the sidewalk, looked in the windows, smiled and waved, then walked on. Lily wasn't gregarious enough to go out and introduce herself, but she smiled and waved back. After receiving a couple calls on her cell phone from friends in Boston, Lily realized that the reception wasn't great, so her next call was to the telephone company to order a phone package for the shop and apartment, including land lines and cell service. The representative promised to send someone out the very next day for installation and activation.

Tate packed up his toolbox and prepared to leave, saying he had work out at the farm to get done. "Will you be okay here on your own?"

"Of course. I'm meeting Miss Mars for lunch in a little while. Then I'll be back here getting ready for the opening."

"That's good. I don't suppose you've met any of the other business owners yet."

"Uh, no. I imagine they're all doing what I'm doing, getting ready for the Grand Opening on Monday."

Tate nodded. "Well, if you need anything, let me know."

Lily smiled and nodded, wishing it was that easy. How many times had she heard her sister, Laurel, say that it was a simple matter of just asking for what you wanted? Lily could never make her outgoing younger sister understand how difficult such a thing was for her.

"Thank you for your help."

"It's what I'm here for."

"Say hi to Isabella for me."

"Sure." He opened the door, the jaunty little bell ringing cheerily, and paused. Looking back over his shoulder, he said, "Look, this isn't Boston. Things move slower here, and there aren't as many conveniences, but the town wants this to work as much as you do. Just give it a chance."

She nodded, and her glasses slid down her nose. "Of course. It'll come together."

"That's the spirit," he told her.

She pushed up her glasses and put on a smile. He went out, leaving her alone. Lily grabbed a screwdriver, and went back to work. Miss Mars came by with a bologna sandwich for lunch, and the two women chatted about some outdoor furniture that Miss Mars thought might make suitable living room furnishings for Lily's apartment. Lily promised to think about it, but then she fixed her mind on arranging supply bins in the workspace behind the scarlet wall so she could start unpacking her boxes and cases. Miss Mars left her to it, and Lily got to work.

When her bell tinkled again, she spun about, expecting Miss Mars or Tate. Someone else stood in the open doorway, however, a slender, petite woman of about sixty. Her short silver-gray hair had been styled to softly frame the strong features of a handsome face that just missed being too long thanks to a bluntly squared chin, prominent cheekbones and large blue eyes. She wore just a touch of mauve eye shadow and a complimentary shade of lipstick. Her tailored pantsuit and pumps marked her as a professional woman, as did the small leather handbag that she clutched to her side.

"Hello," she said, "I'm Coraline Connolly." Then she did the most amazing thing.

She opened her arms, stepped forward and gave Lily something she hadn't even realized she needed. A hug.

Chapter Three

"You must be Lily Farnsworth," Coraline said, reaching up to pat Lily's cheek.

Lily towered over the older woman. Her short stature did not lessen the mantle of authority that she wore like a second skin, however. About sixty, she exuded an aura of unshakeable conviction. Lily bowed her head, pushed up her eyeglasses and smiled.

"A shy one," Coraline Connolly deduced kindly. Lily's startled gaze zipped upward, colliding with Coraline's amused one. "I've seen a thousand just like you, my dear, some too timid to let go of their mothers' skirts on the first day of school, some who didn't look up from their desks for the first week, at least one who didn't speak aloud for a whole year."

"Children," Lily whispered.

"Not all," Coraline refuted. "The last, the one who didn't speak, was the mother of a student." Shocked, Lily blinked. "Shyness can be a burden and a handicap," Coraline went on. "You are not handicapped, I think, but you'll be burdened until you learn to accept yourself as God made you."

Lily drew back at that, not quite sure what to make of it. As usual, she chose to do what she always did when puzzled; she tucked the idea away for perusal later.

"You're a member of the SOS Committee."

"That's right. Welcome to Bygones."

"Thank you. I—I'm glad to be here."

Coraline laughed. "That sounded a bit tentative."

Lily's slender hands fluttered. "Oh, I'm just… That is, I only got here last night, and it's a lot of work. But I'll have everything ready for the opening. I'm sure I will."

Coraline nodded and glanced around. "Is everything to your liking?"

"Oh, yes. I love the shop. And the apartment, too, though it's rather bare right now. But that can wait."

"All right. I assume that Tate Bronson has been in to see you."

"He was here a good part of the morning, actually."

"I see, and did he say when he would return?"

"No, not really."

Coraline nodded thoughtfully before asking, "Do you need anything?"

Lily looked around the shop. What she needed most was encouragement, confidence, but she couldn't very well say so, not even to this kindly woman. She shook her head.

"Well, I won't keep you longer than necessary," Coraline said. "I know how busy you must be, getting ready for next Monday's big event. I just wanted to let you know what the committee has planned for that day."

She went over the details, noting that immediately after Independence Day, the patriotic decorations would come down and the Grand Opening banners would go up. Each of the new businesses would be showcased in a special edition of the *Bygones Gazette,* the local weekly newspaper, on the Friday before the Grand Opening. Following the close of business on that first Monday, the committee would sponsor a reception in the Community Room across the street.

"Tate will be your official host that day."

Lily nodded. "That all sounds great. I have a fresh flower delivery coming on Friday morning, so everything should be in place in plenty of time."

Coraline smiled. "Wonderful. Well, it was nice to meet you."

"You, too," Lily replied, offering her hand. "Come again. Soon."

Instead of shaking hands, Coraline gave her another quick hug. Afterward she tilted her head, asking, "Would you mind if I prayed for you?"

"Not at all," Lily exclaimed, smiling broadly. "Please do."

Coraline patted her cheek again and left her. Lily sighed, pleased. She felt that she had at least two friends now, Miss Ann Mars and Coraline Connolly. It would be stupid of her to wish that she might count Tate Bronson among their number; more than stupid. It would be part of the same unhealthy pattern of the past, part of what she'd left Boston to get away from, what she needed to leave behind and avoid in the future. No, she wouldn't wish to count Tate among her friends, but if it should happen… Turning off that thought, she went back to work.

Miss Mars dropped in on Wednesday with both breakfast and lunch. Others came by to say hello, beginning with the shop owners on either side of Love in Bloom: Melissa Sweeney from the bakery on the corner and Allison True from the bookstore on the other side of the flower shop. Josh Smith went up and down the street distributing cups of coffee from his first official brew. The Cozy Cup Café—on the corner opposite the bakery—was ready for business, he declared, so he stayed to get Lily's computer system operational before moving on to do the same for others. The mayor came by to say hello and welcome her to town, as did the chief of police, Joe Sheridan. Both were members of the SOS Committee.

Whitney Leigh, a serious young reporter with the *Bygones Gazette,* spent a few minutes getting background information for Friday's special edition, but

Lily's stammering answers didn't seem to impress her very much, so she didn't stay long. Other than asking how many years of experience Lily had as a florist and who she thought the mystery benefactor might be behind the grants, Whitney only asked a few questions about the specials Lily intended to offer for the Grand Opening.

Lily knew she shouldn't feel anxious, but she couldn't help it. So much seemed to be riding on this enterprise, and she couldn't help feeling unequal to the task. Even as the others ventured in and out of her shop, she wondered when Tate and Isabella would return. She considered calling Tate to ask his advice on a number of small issues but couldn't bring herself to do it. Instead she got out the paint cans and a brush and tackled the counter.

When Miss Mars closed her shop early and went upstairs, then came down again wearing a hat and gloves with her usual shirtwaist dress, Lily realized that she'd have to do dinner on her own. A moment later an aging but well-kept blue sedan pulled up to the curb, and Miss Mars got inside with another woman. The car drove away, turning left onto Bronson Avenue. Feeling abandoned, Lily gave herself a stern talking-to. She had moved halfway across the country on the basis of a newspaper article. The least she could do now was walk down the street to the grocery store on her own. Determined, she left the shop and set out.

With only three checkout lanes, all currently unmanned, the Hometown Grocery didn't have much to recommend it when compared to the stores in Boston. The fresh produce department would have fit neatly into the bed of a pickup truck, and the butcher department had obviously been shut down, leaving only a single refrigerated case of packaged meats. Lily wandered the aisles virtually alone, without even the company of piped music to mute the squeak of the wheels on the shopping cart. Nevertheless she found all the ingredients for a fine salad, including a small tin of cocktail shrimp and her favorite bottled dressing. She gave up trying to find a suitable bread to eat with it and settled for crackers, thinking that the new bakery was going to do well here. While she was at it, she bought a few things for breakfast and lunch the following day, too.

Knowing that she couldn't carry more, she resisted the urge to buy kitchen gadgets from the selection offered and approached the checkout, surprised to find that a tall thin brunette had materialized from somewhere. The brunette displayed quick efficiency, her thin dark hair scraped back into a tight ponytail.

"You must be the florist."

"Yes. Yes, I am. Lily Farnsworth." She handed over several bills, smiling.

"Heard about you from Tate," said the brunette, making change.

"Oh?"

This elicited a nod as the woman began bagging the groceries.

Lily couldn't help wondering just what Tate had said or where he was keeping himself, for that matter. She thought he was supposed to be her host.

"Where is everyone?" she asked tentatively.

"Wednesday evening," the woman replied, as if that was answer enough. When Lily just blinked at her, she added, "Most folks are in church for midweek service."

"Ah."

"Folks don't have midweek service back in Boston?"

"Some do, yes." But Lily's church had not.

"Hereabouts, nearly everyone goes to midweek service," the checker said. "We rotate shifts here at the grocery so no one has to miss the service more than once a month."

"I see."

"Folks in Boston must eat shrimp," the checker commented cheerfully, pushing the bags toward Lily.

"Yes, we…*they* do," Lily said, gathering up the bags. "Boston is known for its seafood."

The brunette smiled. "That's good. Maybe I can move those cans back there now."

Lily glanced down at her groceries and nodded. Canned shrimp and midweek service. Well, it was a start. She had the makings of a reasonable meal and a good explanation for the empty aisles. She liked the thought of a churchgoing community. She'd been the odd man out for as long as she could remember, the one who didn't fit, even among her own family. Maybe it would be different here.

Lily slept in the next morning, it being a national holiday. She expected some sort of community Independence Day celebration, but when none had materialized by midmorning, she went downstairs and got busy. Miss Mars came up with a suggestion. Lily doubted it could work at first. Even if the flowers arrived precisely on schedule the next day, she didn't have the resources to do as the lady proposed.

"You can find what you need in my shop," Miss Mars insisted. "Just use your imagination."

Lily shrugged doubtfully. "First I would need to visit the other businesses."

"Of course. That's no problem. I think everyone is doing just what you are today."

How could Lily refuse to try after that? Leaving her shop unlocked—as Miss Mars pointed out, they would be within "shouting distance" all the time— they went from shop to shop, starting with the Sweet Dreams Bakery on the corner. Miss Mars was right. All the newcomers were hard at work.

Melissa Sweeney could not have been sweeter or more enthusiastic, and her shop gave Lily lots of ideas. Melissa eagerly accepted the offer of the loan of a floral arrangement to decorate her counter for the Grand Opening. Josh Smith, at the Cozy Cup

Café, who struck Lily as a bit of a computer geek, did the same, as did Allison True at the Happy Endings Bookstore, Patrick Fogerty of The Fixer-Upper hardware store and Chase Rollins at Fluff & Stuff, the pet shop.

The problem remained supplies, but Lily did as Miss Mars advised and combed through the back room of the This 'N' That, with happy results. Not only did she find some wonderful containers—a tin bread box, an old typewriter, a battered percolator, a bird cage, an antique vase and a rusty length of pipe, as well as a pair of old cowboy boots and the hat to go with them—she even found some usable silk flowers. She also discovered several bits of furniture that she could use in her apartment. In fact, the outdoor stuff that Miss Mars wanted her to consider didn't look very "outdoorsy" at all. Rattan with red cushions about the same shade of scarlet as the short wall in her workroom, the three-piece set might work out just fine.

Lily took the lot and got it all at a very good price. At least Miss Mars was seeing some profit from the SOS project. Hauling as much of her newly found treasures over to her place as she could, Lily discovered that she had company.

"Lily!" Isabella cried. Dressed in patriotic garb, she rushed forward to throw her arms around Lily's waist as if they were old, dear friends. "Happy Independence Day!"

Lily laughed, juggling armfuls of treasures. "Hello. How good to see you. How have you been?"

"Fine. Your shop looks pretty." Isabella obviously liked the lavender counter and the little scarlet heart dotting the *i* in the shop logo.

"I'm guessing that your favorite color is purple," Lily said, depositing her goods on the countertop, but Isabella shook her head.

"Pink!"

"Really?" Lily brushed off her hands, smiling. "I'll remember that."

Tate, whom Lily had tried hard not to notice too keenly, made an impatient sound. "Where have you been? We've been waiting here for twenty minutes."

Lily's delight at seeing them diminished. "I'm sorry. Miss Mars came up with a plan for me to make floral arrangements for each of the new shops to use as decorations for the Grand Opening, but I had to find the right containers. And look! Just look at what we found."

She started describing how she would use each of her treasures. "What could be better for the Fluff & Stuff than a bird cage? Right? I'm thinking blues and greens and yellows. We'll hang it right next to that cheeky parrot of his. And the percolator will work great for the coffee shop. Not sure about those flowers, maybe some 'chocolaty' reds. With a little paint, the bread box will make a beautiful display for the bakery next door. All pastels there. Oh, my favorite is an antique typewriter. That's still across the street. It's sooo heavy, but how perfect is that for a bookstore? Plus, I'm finally going to have furni—"

"So you're going to do all this and still be ready for the opening?" Tate interrupted sharply.

Stung, Lily bowed her head. "Yes, I—I think so. If I have some help."

Tate stepped back, and Lily cringed inwardly. "I'm sorry. I—I didn't mean to imply... That is...I suppose I am a bit overwhelmed, but when Miss Mars suggested that flower arrangements for all the shops would be a good way to showcase my design abilities and dress up the shops for the Grand Opening, too..." Lily sighed and shook her head. "Perhaps I'm not as forceful as I should be. I've always been a bit shy, and..." She let the words dwindle away, uncertain where she was even going with this.

Tate cleared his throat and mumbled something about being worried when he'd found the shop empty and not wanting to overburden her when she was trying to get the place together.

In the midst of the awkward silence that followed, Isabella piped up with "You were wrong, Dad, and Mrs. Connolly was right."

Tate speared her with a pointed glance. "Duh."

"Just saying," Isabella went on, shrugging.

Lily looked from one to the other of them in confusion.

Tate rolled his eyes and admitted, "Coraline came to see me, okay? She thought you needed help and wanted to organize a work brigade, but I assumed you were doing okay and we just needed to stay out of your way." He looked aside, adding, "You appeared to be getting things together. Others seemed to need more help."

Lily had to admit that, from what she'd seen just today, a bakery, coffee shop, bookstore, pet shop and hardware store all required significantly more preparation than a floral shop. "You have a point there. I'm the problem. I—I haven't been as focused as I need to be. Frankly, being from Boston, I'm used to having more people around." Most of whom would actually speak to her without waiting for her to speak first.

Tate rubbed a hand over his head. "Well, about that, the committee sort of asked the townspeople to leave all you newcomers alone until you get set up and settled."

Lily straightened. "What?" They had actually asked people to leave her alone?

"We had to," he argued. "Otherwise, they'd have been all over you on day one with covered dishes and dinner invitations."

Lily smiled. "Really?"

"We had to turn down every civic group in town to keep them from plastering you all with invitations to join everything from the Quilting Club to the Birthday Lunch Bunch."

"Seriously?"

"You name it, you're going to get hit up to join it. Soon."

"Oh. That's…that's nice."

He gave her a crooked smile. "You can tell me later if you still think that's nice."

"No, really, I was looking forward to the sense of community that you always hear about in a small town. In fact, I was hoping for a community-wide Independence Day celebration."

"Not this year," Tate said grimly. "The city had to decide between that and the Grand Opening reception."

"And they decided on the reception?"

"It seemed more important."

Lily took that in. "Wow." This thing was even more vital than she'd realized.

"We got some fireworks at home for later tonight," Isabella told her, cutting her eyes at her father.

Tate cleared his throat. "Right now, though, we have work to do." He clapped his hands together. "So what's first?"

Lily shook her head. "Oh, you don't have to—"

"What's first?" he interrupted firmly.

Biting her lips against a smile, she shrugged. "I bought a lot of stuff from Miss Mars, and it's got to get over here somehow. Some of it's pretty big."

"I'll pull my truck around the back of her store."

"Thank you."

"No problem," he said. "Isabella, let's go."

She shook her curly red head. "I'll stay here and help Lily."

"Sure," Lily agreed quickly. "I've got bins to fill in the workroom. Spools and spools of ribbon to line up."

"I like ribbon," Isabella declared.

Lily grinned down at her. "I thought you might."

Tate paused, but then he nodded. "Okay. We'll finish those display shelves next."

"Wonderful."

He went off to fetch the rest of her purchases, leaving Lily and Isabella to unpack and arrange spools of ribbon according to color and width. When he returned, Lily helped him carry the furniture up to the apartment. She had something to sit on now, as well as a bedside table and a lamp. Later she would paint the rattan the same shade, hopefully, as the cushions and accessorize with a contrasting color, perhaps a rich yellow gold. She couldn't think of that now, though. Instead she hurried back downstairs with Tate to get to work in the shop. The time flew by; she barely seemed to have time to think, and as the shop took shape, her excitement and her hope grew.

Only as Isabella began to flag, her little tummy rumbling, did Lily stop to take stock. That's when she realized how much this one man and his sweet little daughter had accomplished for her. How could she not like them, *him,* just a little then? How could she not count them among her friends? Even if the relationship was predicated on business, they could still be friends, couldn't they? So long as she didn't let herself think of him as anything more than that, everything would be fine.

"I'm hungry."

Tate tightened the last screw, stepped back and glanced at his wrist. "Is that the time? No wonder you're hungry, honey. Wow. Where'd the day go?"

"Time flies when you're having fun," Lily quipped, getting up off the floor. Tate chuckled. She seemed to spend half her time on the floor— and the other half shoving her glasses back up her nose. He couldn't help smiling and shaking his head.

"I think we've made good progress," Tate said, putting away the screwdriver.

"We have, indeed," she agreed. "Thank you both. Very much."

"You're welcome. Now we really have to get going."

"I understand. If I don't run, I won't make it to the grocery before it closes."

He made a face. "The store closed early for the holiday."

She bowed her head. "I should have thought of that."

"You can have dinner with us," Isabella instantly invited. "Right, Dad? We got lots of leftovers from our barbecue at Grandma's house today."

Lifting her head, Lily blinked at Tate, and he

blinked back. He couldn't very well leave her without dinner, and he needed to get home sooner rather than later.

"Tell you what, we'll pick up some burgers at The Everything on the way out to our place. I saw they were open today, and I have to get home to feed the livestock. It's not far, so I can just drive you back in later after the fireworks."

Obviously surprised, Lily hesitated. He found himself holding his breath until she smiled and nodded, which made no sense at all, except that Isabella would have been disappointed, of course.

"Okay. Do I have time to run upstairs first?"

"Sure. I can lock up here and get Isabella into the truck."

"Great." She handed over the keys and hurried out.

He turned off lights, locked the doors, ignored his daughter's none-too-subtle babbling about how much she liked Lily and belted the matchmaking little magpie into her booster seat.

"She has pretty hair and eyes and hands," Isabella said, "and she's very nice, too."

"That's enough now," he told her firmly. "I don't want to hear any more about it. Understand?" Isabella nodded, but he'd seen that look in her eye before. "I mean it. I don't have time for a girlfriend."

"If you had a wife—"

"I had a wife," Tate reminded Isabella softly. "I don't want another." She quieted finally, and he pulled out his cell phone, saying casually, "I'm going to call ahead and order our burgers now, but this is not a date. It's just a nice thing to do for someone new in town on a holiday. Got it?"

"Got it."

He doubted that, but he tapped his daughter on the end of her button nose and closed the truck door.

Lily came skipping down the stairs a couple minutes later in skinny jeans, athletic shoes and a snug red T-shirt.

Tate tried not to gulp, but he had the sudden feeling that he'd just made a very big mistake.

Chapter Four

"I, uh, called ahead for the burgers," Tate managed, trying not to stare. "Ordered yours with everything but cheese. So, uh, that way you can take anything off the burger that you don't want."

Lily smiled that soft smile that did funny things to his insides and said, "That's fine."

"I ordered the condiments on the side, too."

"Okay."

He wanted to kick himself. Instead he said, "Let's go then."

He opened the passenger door for her, then wished he hadn't because of the way she smiled and the way that smile made him feel. Lily hopped inside the truck, and Tate hurried around to do the same and start up the engine.

The street was deserted, so he hooked a U-turn, came to a stop at the four-way and turned left onto Bronson. Half a block later, he turned left again, bringing the truck to a stop in front of the L-shaped building across from the school.

"Interesting building," Lily commented.

Tate chuckled. "If by *interesting* you mean cobbled together from an old house, a shed and a gas station."

"Why is it called The Everything?"

"Well, it's part convenience store, part grill and part gas station, which was just about everything we needed around here at the time."

"What are the picnic tables for?"

"Extra seating, and it gives the local teens someplace to hang out even when the grill is closed. Velma Dill, one of the proprietors, sometimes nukes frozen pizzas for them. Her husband, Elwood, is one of the SOS Committee members. You'll meet them at the reception after the Grand Opening."

"He's the one with the beard," Isabella put in from the backseat.

Tate chuckled. "It's a joke. The Dills are self-proclaimed hippies, the long-haired sort, in their early 50s, both with visible tattoos, earrings and headscarves. They basically dress and look pretty much alike."

"But Elwood has a beard, I take it," Lily surmised.

"A long, scraggly one. He's actually a pretty good guy. Gives gasoline to folks who can't pay, and there are a lot of those around since Randall shut down the plant."

"I read about that," Lily said.

"The Dills have really stepped up since Randall Manufacturing closed," Tate told her. "We try to give them as much business as we can. They're open today so folks who can't afford to cook out can get burgers at half price."

Lily nodded. "Good to know. I don't have a car, but the store is certainly convenient, and a girl's gotta eat. I'll be sure to give them my business."

Smiling, Tate went in and picked up the burgers and fries while Lily and Isabella waited in the truck. As he climbed back in a few minutes later, he heard his daughter saying, "And Dad doesn't ever do anything fun."

Imagining what else she'd said, Tate reached into the bag and took out a cardboard cup of fries, passing them back to her, along with a bottle of water. "Here. Eat these." That ought to keep her little mouth busy.

Instead of heading on down Bronson Avenue and then taking a left on Church Street, Tate chose to head east on School Drive. That way Lily got to see Bronson Park, with its pretty pond, gazebo and playground. They turned back south on Granary Road and passed by the old Bronson Homestead. The house now contained the Public Library. Behind the Homestead, on property donated by the Bronsons, stood Bygones Community Church, which fronted on the aptly named Church Street. They passed a few residential streets and then drove over a cattle guard onto Bronson property.

"So it's the city limit on one side and your place on the other," Lily clarified. "You're practically in town then."

"Nope. House is still a mile or so away."

She lifted her eyebrows at that, quipping, "This is quite a yard you've got here."

He chuckled. "You could say that. It's part of the original holdings. My folks' house is about a half mile east of mine. We're country folk. Wouldn't know how to get along in town."

"I'm a city girl," she said. "Bygones doesn't really feel like town to me."

"All a matter of perspective, I guess," he said.

"Yes, it is," she agreed, looking around her.

He tried to see it as she did, the wide-open spaces, the fields gilded by the rising moon. It looked like peace to him. It looked like the whole world. It looked like home. He hadn't prayed in a long while, but if he was going to pray, he would ask God to make this crazy scheme to save Bygones work out, for Lily Farnsworth's sake as much as anyone's.

Nothing Lily had seen thus far had prepared her for what she found at the end of the road. She had already discovered that the topography of the plains was deceptive. Though seemingly flat as pancakes, they were, in fact, low undulating hills, wherein lay small hidden valleys, so that what looked like shrubs in the distance gradually became trees tucked into broad, rolling folds. It came as no surprise then that, as they topped a shallow rise, a wide shady hollow spread out before them. No, the surprise was in how Tate had adapted his home to the natural beauty of his glade.

Lily's gaze fell first on the barn in a field of golden, knee-high grass. Constructed in the shape of a large rectangle, the building's walls of native stone supported the weight of its steep sheet-metal roof, while the upper diamond-shaped end walls were made of wood painted a deep, rich red. Corrals of stone, wood and metal pipe surrounded the barn, as well as several smaller outbuildings of the same dark red.

The two-story house mirrored the barn in construction, with the lower walls built of native stone and the upper portion of cedar planking stained a deep red. Even the roof was made of shiny corrugated sheet metal and extended to cover a deep porch that surrounded the house on three sides. The builder had somehow managed to tuck the house, which couldn't have been more than ten years old yet managed to seem ageless, into a grove of mature hickory trees. Stone walkways completed the picture.

The whole place seemed to have emerged naturally from its surroundings, as if everything had grown there organically. God might have designed the land for these buildings. Certainly, whoever had designed the buildings had done so with the land in mind. To Lily's thinking, the only thing the place lacked was flowers.

She wouldn't have planted formal gardens. They would have looked out of place and ruined the natural ambience. Instead she would have added a rosebush here or there, and some hanging pots of flowers, a splash of color to draw the eye. She couldn't think of another thing that she might have added, especially when she saw the rocking chairs and swing on the porch.

"It's beautiful, Tate," she whispered reverently, "just beautiful."

He tossed her a smile as he guided the truck around a curve in the pebbled drive and toward the back of the house. "Thanks. It's been a work in progress." He glanced into the rearview mirror, addressing his daughter. "Pumpkin, will you take Lily and the food into the house? I need to get to the barn."

"Sure, Daddy."

"Can I help?" Lily asked.

He brought the truck to a halt in front of the open garage. "Ever feed livestock?"

"No, but I'm willing to learn."

He turned to look at Isabella in the backseat. "What about you, Buttercup?"

"I'll show Lily what to do."

"Okay, then."

He backed the truck out and headed for the barn. Two minutes later they were walking along a graveled path. Tate closed a gate at the back of the barn then went into a small room just inside the building.

"Open the stall doors. We have an automatic feed and water system for the horses that I can activate in here. We'll have to feed the cattle up front by hand after I drive in the horses."

Isabella showed Lily how to slide the gates open. They would have to quickly roll them closed again after the horses were inside. Once the automatic feed system started dumping grain into the bins, Tate grabbed a rope and walked out to one of the corrals. Soon hooves thundered through the barn. Isabella hopped up on a post and advised Lily to climb up behind her. Perhaps a dozen different horses swung into six stalls and dropped their noses into feed bins. Isabella plopped down to the straw strewn floor and started whisking the gates closed. Lily followed suit. Tate jogged up, coiling his rope, and helped finish the job.

He slung the rope over one shoulder and returned to the small room at the back of the building, reappearing a few moments later with a laden wheelbarrow. The girls followed him to a pen at the front of the barn. While Isabella and, belatedly, Lily, dumped feed into a bucket, Tate crawled over a fence and dropped a loop over the head of a good-size calf, which he then snugged to a post.

"Sugar, bring me the kit," he said, running a hand down the calf's flank to its belly. Isabella picked up a black zippered bag and handed it to Lily, who then carried it over to Tate. "Grab his tail," he instructed, "but watch those back legs and don't get yourself kicked."

"Uh. Okay."

He glanced up in surprise at Lily then shot his daughter a speaking glance before turning his attention back to the calf. "Pull on his tail. Just stay well back while I doctor him."

Lily looked at Isabella, who nodded encouragingly, and grabbed hold of the swishing tail, stepping back and leaning away from the animal. It jerked and bawled, but Lily held on, reasoning that if Isabella could manage such a feat then she surely could. Crouching down next to the animal, Tate crooned a steady stream of encouraging words as he unzipped the kit, prepared a syringe and then irrigated a wound on the calf's underside, explaining his actions as he went along. The animal didn't really put up much of a fight. Apparently it had been through this process several times already. Tate ended by giving the ungrateful beast an injection, then he waved Lily away, released the calf's head and chuckled as it trotted to the bucket to feed.

He and Lily walked to the fence. After helping her climb over, he passed the medical kit to Isabella and easily vaulted the fence himself. Lily and Isabella sat in the truck while Tate tossed bales of hay into the back before driving around to the corral in front. He cut the wire on the bales, and the three of them tossed the hay into the corral to feed the few head of cattle penned there for one reason or another.

They scrubbed their hands at a spigot beside the barn, using a bar of soap inside a net hanging by a chain, and ate their burgers sitting on the tailgate of the truck while the sky darkened and the stars began to pop out.

She said a quick, silent prayer of thanks for the meal, as was her habit, and took a bite. *Now this,* Lily thought, breathing deeply of the loamy smells of earth and animals and growing things, *is more like it.* While nothing at all like what she had imagined, this was somehow what she had been seeking when she'd filled out her grant application back in Boston. Strangely she finally felt that she was getting to know Bygones and Kansas. Or maybe it was that she was getting to know Tate and Isabella.

"Grandma and Grandpa will be here with the fireworks soon," Tate observed, after chugging the last of his water and recapping the bottle.

"Time to strain the berry tea!" Isabella announced excitedly.

They climbed into the truck and drove to the house. This time Tate pulled into the neatly organized garage and everyone got out. Isabella led the way, chattering all the while about the special tea that had been steeping all day.

"It's a berry special recipe," she joked. "It come down in the family. We get the berries as soon as they're dark enough. They grow practically on the ground, so you got to watch where you're stepping, and when we get enough I boil 'em up with the leaves. Daddy helps me. And we cook the sugar in until you can't even see it anymore. When it's not hot, we put it in the fridge, and then after a long time, I pour it through a piece of material. What is it, Daddy?"

"Cheesecloth."

"Oh, yeah. I don't know why it's called that, 'cause we don't make cheese. We're making tea, blue tea for Red, White and Blue Day! It's tadition."

"*Tra*dition," Tate corrected patiently.

"Yep. Tadition, from my grandma Hoyt to my mama to me. Daddy says it's his favorite thing about the whole day."

Lily looked around her as they passed through a tiled back hall that opened onto the rear yard at one end and into the front entry, flanking the stairwell, at the other. Hooks bearing various outer garments lined the wall on either side of the door into the garage. A box bench, no doubt containing galoshes and other types of footwear, stood between the back and garage doors, its hinged seat painted with daisies. An old-fashioned milk can sat next to it, filled with umbrellas, a baseball bat and a scarred cane. The whole thing had a neat but homey feel to it. More telling than any of that, however, were the photos lining the opposite wall.

All eight-by-tens in identical wood frames, they varied between photos of a chubby, bright-eyed, flame-haired infant and an equally bright-eyed, flame-haired young woman whose curls tumbled down her slender back in wild abandon, or were sometimes tamed into twin French braids that ringed her head and frothed into a riot of curls at her nape. The redheaded beauty yelled at a base-ball game, petted a horse, laughed heartily, smiled dreamily, sat on a log, drove a tractor... The baby, no doubt Isabella, played with her toes, a favorite rattle, a doll, reached for a mobile, blew bubbles at the camera. There were no photos of the two of them together, no photos of Tate or anyone else, just Isabella and the young woman who had to be her mother.

The latter woke an ache in Lily's chest. She had the feeling that she was looking at the reason for Tate's every frown, snap and growl.

Daddy's not married, either.

Lily had tried not to think about Isabella's state-ment, not to wonder how Tate had come to be a single father, but she felt in her bones that he was not divorced. No, these photos told her that Tate Bronson was widowed. Somehow his young wife had died. He had yet, however, to let her go. That became abundantly clear as Lily followed father and daughter into the roomy kitchen with its golden woods and rusty stone countertops.

While Lily sat at an iron and glass table, Tate and Isabella fetched a pot from the stainless steel refrig-erator, fastened a piece of cheesecloth over a crock in the sink and slowly poured the contents of the pot into the crock. From where Lily sat, she could see through the dining room to the living area, where a large, gilt-framed wedding portrait hung. A very young Tate in cowboy hat, blue jeans and a tuxedo jacket ran hand-in-hand with Isabella's mother, who wore a billowing, strapless white wedding gown, her long, curly red hair and a white veil flowing out behind them, across a field of golden waving grass much like that which surrounded the barn outside. Sunlight slanted across a cloudless sky, beaming down on the happy couple.

Lily's heart literally ached for him. What had happened? How had Tate survived such loss? She felt silly and foolish, remembering her distress when some man she'd liked had failed to notice her or, worse, had shown an interest in her more vivacious younger sister. Tate had truly loved. Tate had been loved. His loss had been real. Lily's had never been more than secret and imagined.

God forgive me for my petty self-centeredness, she prayed silently.

A giggle drew her attention back to the activities at the sink. The cloth was now piled with berries and leaves. Tate set aside the pot and twisted the cloth to remove all the juice before dumping the remains into the compost can, then he stretched a fresh piece of clean white cloth over the top of the crock. He did this twice more before the pot was empty. Isabella's fingers were stained by the time they were done, but thanks to a dishtowel that Tate had draped around her neck, her clothing remained clean. Tate squirted dishwashing liquid into the pot and ran hot water into it then left it to sit while he and Isabella filled glasses with ice and ran the tea from a spigot in the crock. Isabella then proudly presented a glass to Lily. The tea was indeed blue, sweet and a bit minty.

"Lovely. What is it?"

"Dewberry," Tate answered. "It was Eve's grandmother's recipe."

She didn't have to ask who "Eve" might be, not that she had a chance as the front door opened and a middle-aged couple entered, followed by a younger couple and a toddler. Tate introduced Lily to his parents. Ginny and Peter Bronson were both in their fifties. Ginny's short, thick, ash-blond hair hid her silvering well, but Peter's dark brown showed a liberal sprinkling of gray. Tate obviously got his dimples from his dad and his warm brown eyes from his mom, from whom he also apparently got his height, Peter standing little more than an inch taller than his wife. The young brunette and tall, dark-haired man with the lopsided nose turned out to be Tate's older sister, Gayla, and her husband, Bud Lott, visiting from Kansas City with their two-year-old son, Jay. Everyone seemed surprised to find Lily there, but no one appeared unhappy about it.

"You're one of the newcomers," Ginny Bronson said.

"That's right."

"Well, don't worry," Gayla, Tate's sister, quipped, "just because the whole town's future is resting on your shoulders."

"The whole town?" Lily echoed, alarmed. Was the situation in Bygones truly that dire?

"Oh, not you personally," Gayla said with a contrived little wave. "Besides, I hear that everyone has great hopes for this scheme." She quickly changed the subject then, almost as full of questions as Isabella, though she managed to be a bit more subtle than Isabella had been.

Everyone exclaimed about Isabella's berry tea, which they all drank while eating heaping helpings of Ginny Bronson's flag cake, a confection topped with whipped cream, strawberries and blueberries. The Fourth of July, Peter Bronson joked, was always a "berry good time."

After the cake they all trouped outside, carrying folding lawn chairs, and up to the crest of a low hill behind the house overlooking a pond, where a space had been cleared. Peter opened a box, and the fun began with Tate and Bud, who were obviously good friends, setting off the fireworks. Jay sat in his grandfather's lap, while Isabella sat in her grandmother's, oohing and aahing over every bang and bright splash of color. By the time the last starburst drifted into the dark mirror of the pond, Jay snored on his grandpa's shoulder and Isabella's eyelids drooped, though how either could entertain the notion of sleep with all the noise was beyond Lily's understanding.

As the party walked back to the house, Peter talked about his forebears. "This was all part of the original homestead of Saul Bronson," he said. "He came to the state in 1870 from St. Louis."

"Isabella said something about a disagreement over a girlfriend," Lily ventured warily.

"Mmm-hmm. Sarabeth DeMonde. Both Paul and Saul courted her, but she chose Paul, prompting Saul to head west and lose himself out here on the prairie. Within a few months, though, Paul realized that Sarabeth was not worth losing his brother and only family over. He followed Saul to Kansas, and together the brothers founded the town, calling it Bygones in keeping with Saul's decision to forgive and forget. The brothers enjoyed a sizable inheritance from their parents, who were in shipping, and converted it into land. Eventually both married. Saul and his wife lived in town. Paul and his family preferred the country. Guess we take after Paul."

"I can see why," she said, inhaling deeply, enjoying the relative quiet. A bird called in the distance, the sound haunting and strangely poignant. "What is that?"

"Whip-poor-will," Tate answered. "I sit out here sometimes at night and listen to them for hours. Don't know which I love more, them or the doves."

"It's that old owl around here that I love to hear,"

Ginny said. "I go to sleep listening to that 'hoo-hoo-hoo.'"

"I've got a sleepy baby bird right here," Bud said, cradling his son against his chest.

"We'd better get back to the house and get him down for the night," Gayla said.

"We'll be along shortly," Peter told them as they moved off toward their vehicle.

"Mom," Tate said, "could you stay and get Isabella to bed while I run Lily back into town?"

"Of course, son. Your dad can ride on home with Gayla and Bud."

"Thanks, I appreciate it."

Isabella hugged Lily, saying a sleepy "G'night."

"Good night, sweetie, and thank you for all the help today and the yummy tea and the invitation. I had a *berry* good time."

Isabella giggled and went with her grandparents into the house. "It was nice to meet you, Lily," Ginny called as she passed through the door held open by her husband.

"You, too. Good night."

Tate walked her into the dark garage and opened the truck door for her again, handing her up into the passenger seat of the cab with exquisite care. Lily read that as accurately as a letter.

Dear Lily, I will treat you as you deserve to be treated. Please do not mistake it for anything more than common courtesy. Sincerely, Tate Bronson.

She thought of all those photos on the walls of his

home and felt like crying, as much for herself as for him—not that she was foolish enough to think of Tate Bronson as anything other than a nice young man who had been dealt a heavy blow. She just hated for any of her friends to carry around the kind of sadness she now sensed in him.

Chapter Five

Lily Farnsworth was a quiet one. Well, quieter than the other women of his acquaintance, anyway, Tate mused. She was quieter than his mom, way quieter than Gayla, quieter than Eve had been or certainly Isabella would ever be. Tate had seen her looking at the photos, and he knew that she wanted to ask questions, but she wouldn't. He could avoid the whole subject just by keeping his own mouth shut. The puzzling thing was that, for once, he didn't want to avoid the subject.

He waited until the house fell from sight in his rearview mirror, then he just said it.

"She died of a stroke about four minutes after Isabella was born."

Lily gasped, her face turning to him so that the dash lights reflected off the lenses of her glasses. "What?"

"Eve. My wife. She died about four minutes after Isabella was born."

"Oh, my."

"It was a long, difficult labor," he went on. "Eve's blood pressure had spiked repeatedly, but the doctor wasn't worried. Then we went into delivery. Evie was so tired. I said, 'Let's get this over with, sweetheart. Let's bring our little girl into the world.' I don't know how she did it. She pushed so hard, and then there was Isabella, beautiful and perfect. We were laughing and holding her together while the doctor and nurses took care of things, and then they asked Eve for one more push. Suddenly she convulsed. Her eyes rolled back in her head, and she died in the space of a heartbeat."

"Tate." Lily reached across the cab and latched onto his forearm with her finely knuckled hand. "I'm so sorry."

He nodded, feeling oddly comforted. "They tried to bring her back. They knew she'd stroked, that her brain was gone, but they'd hoped to keep her heart beating so she wouldn't die on our daughter's birthday, but it didn't work."

Lily took her hand back. "I don't know what to say."

"Nothing to say. Eve and I were high school sweethearts. We married young. Everyone thought too young, but we were sensible and got our house built and in order before we started our family. And then Eve was gone."

"Your greatest joy and deepest sorrow within minutes," Lily whispered.

He nodded. "That about sums it up. A father and a widower on the same day. I don't think I'd have made it through the loss without my daughter."

"I'm glad you have her."

"So am I, but you can see now why Isabella latches on to every single woman of a motherly age who crosses her path."

"Because she never knew her own mother."

"Just so. Make no mistake about it, though." He shifted in his seat and said it straight out. "I never intend to remarry."

"But marrying again doesn't mean that you'd be widowed again."

"How do you know?"

"Well, I don't *know,* but the odds against it are—"

"The odds against it the first time were high."

"Still—"

"I won't marry again because I won't have more children," Tate stated flatly. "I can't go through that again. I just won't risk it," he told her, "and no one has a right to ask me to. No one. Not after what I've been through."

"O-of course," Lily whispered, ducking her head.

Tate nodded, telling himself that it had to be said. It was better this way. Now, no one would be hurt. No one would start imagining futures where none could exist. They could be friends without worrying about romantic foolishness.

He changed the subject, chatting about fireworks and dewberry tea, the calf he'd treated and the progress they'd made in the shop that day. She nodded, hummed and tried to act interested, but he felt like Isabella, running off at the mouth. When they got to the shop, he started to get out and go around to open her door for her, but she hopped out before he could get a boot on the ground.

"Thank you for a lovely evening," she called from the curb. "And for all your help this afternoon."

"Sure," he replied, waving. "No problem."

She closed the door. As he pulled away, he heard her say something. It sounded like "Just part of your official responsibilities."

Why that made him squirm, he didn't know. It was only the truth. He was her SOS Committee contact and host. Nothing more. He had done what he was supposed to do where she was concerned, and now that he'd laid out the facts, he could fulfill his official responsibilities without fear of any misunderstandings between them. Finally he could relax around her. He was sure that he'd start to feel good about that anytime now.

Staring down at the dark, empty street the next evening, Lily set aside her prepackaged dinner, her meal largely untouched. Earlier that morning after her flowers had arrived, she had worked on the arrangements that she had promised the other business owners, pouring everything she had into the work, aware that much depended on the success of this "scheme," as Gayla had put it. Throughout the afternoon the Independence Day decorations had come down, and the Grand Opening banner had gone up. Spanning the street, it declared Monday as the "Heart of Main Street GRAND OPENING" and named the new businesses in town: Cozy Cup Café, Sweet Dreams Bakery, Love in Bloom, Happy Endings Bookstore, The Fixer-Upper and Fluff & Stuff. Spurred by that reminder of the looming opening and the hopes of the town, Lily had stayed so busy that she'd barely had time to think about Tate or Isabella or the previous evening's events. Yet everything he'd told her had hovered in the back of her mind.

She had held it off by hurrying to the grocery to fully stock her freezer, refrigerator and pantry, paying to have what she couldn't carry, including numerous cans of tiny shrimp, delivered by a teenage boy in a beat-up Jeep. Now, however, with the day done and downtown all but deserted, she could no longer hold the shadows at bay. Instead she let the dark clouds roll over the horizon of her thoughts and faced facts.

She was a fool when it came to men. She continually built emotional castles in the air around men who cared nothing for her. Most had never known she even existed. Tate, at least, had recognized her interest. He'd seen that she was intrigued by him and his daughter, despite her best intentions and better judgment, and he'd let her know that she shouldn't pin any hopes on him. She should be grateful to him, not moping around and disappointed.

Lily stared across the street at the yellow light behind the window shade of Miss Mars's apartment and wondered if she would still be here in another fifty or sixty years, sitting alone, eating frozen dinners and staring down at an empty street. If so, she hoped she would be as good-natured and sweet about it as Miss Mars. Lily couldn't help wondering if that old dear had ever had her silly heart broken. Did she have a sister, for instance, who had married the man with whom she'd fancied herself in love? Lily could not even call home to Boston for fear of hearing about the newlyweds, who were no doubt back from the honeymoon by now and at the law firm, taking the world by storm. No, it was better to sit alone and concentrate on what was important.

This town was important. Making her business a success was important. Living the life that God had ordained for her was important. That mattered most of all.

After a while Lily went to her room, got out her Bible and read until her eyes grew heavy and she finally slept, comforted. For the moment at least.

She woke the next morning uneasy, however, and no matter how industriously she worked, for some reason Lily couldn't seem to pull the shop together. Oh, all the elements were there. The fixtures were all in place. The fresh flowers had been delivered. The painting had been finished and the shelves were stocked, but the place seemed a jumble. Lily couldn't put her finger on what was wrong, so she simply asked God to show her what was missing.

After saying that prayer, she decided to spend the majority of Saturday afternoon finishing the arrangements and delivering them to the various stores. Everyone seemed quite pleased, and she tried to take heart from that. Feeling that she had done all that she could, Lily spent the evening painting her furniture and puttering around the apartment. She went to bed that evening pleasantly exhausted— and woke the following morning deeply depressed.

She missed her friends. She missed her church. She missed her old apartment, dinky and expensive as it had been. She missed her *car,* as pathetic as that seemed. Everything just felt all wrong, and this being Sunday, she didn't even have the distraction of work to occupy her mind. Worry moved in and took up residence.

What if she couldn't make the shop a success? Bygones was banking on her and the others to make their businesses work. Suddenly it felt as if the town expected too much, needed too much. Lily knew, of course, that such defeatist thoughts were not of God and that she should get her mind off them.

An image of the church by which Tate had driven her on Thursday came to her, and Lily briefly considered walking there. It couldn't be more than six or seven blocks, but she hadn't noted the service times so didn't know when to arrive. Besides, she'd never been bold enough to walk into any place un-invited and unannounced all alone.

Well, she would just have to have church by her-self. So determined, she made herself presentable, fetched her Bible from her bedroom, perched on the chaise, which was quickly becoming her preferred piece of furniture and began to read aloud from the eighth Psalm.

"'O Lord, our Lord, how majestic is your name in all the earth! You have set your glory above the heavens.'"

A tapping came at her door, and she looked up from the Bible as if expecting a guest to material-ize in the center of the room. But of course she had locked her door the night before. It was easier to take the girl out of Boston than to take Boston out of the girl, after all. Keeping her finger inside the Bible to hold her place, she quickly rose and moved into the tiny entry to let in her guest.

Miss Ann Mars hopped into the room like a bent, white-haired sparrow, wearing hat and gloves. "Hurry now," she admonished gently, smiling at the Bible in Lily's hands. "We'll be late for church."

"Oh! How did you know? Th-that I'd want to go, I mean."

Miss Mars smiled and took the Bible from her hands. "An old lady learns to notice things, like how a certain someone always prays over her meals. Quickly now."

Laughing, Lily ran to pull on her best dress, a

soft navy blue floral print with a hem that frothed inches above her ankles. She tossed a long slender lavender scarf about her neck. As she stepped into flat shoes, Miss Mars called out that she'd meet Lily downstairs. Grabbing her keys and handbag from the bedside table, Lily softly sang the words that she had read earlier.

"'O Lord, our Lord, how majestic is your name in all the earth…'"

Even in Kansas.

The back driver's-side door of the familiar blue sedan stood open. Lily reached inside and laid her Bible, with its soft dark red-leather binding, on the seat. Coraline Connolly twisted to look over her shoulder from the driver's seat. Miss Mars had taken the front passenger side.

"Thank you so much for the ride," Lily said, slipping into the car. "I've seen you stopping for Miss Mars before."

Coraline chuckled. "I've been picking up Ann for services at the Bygones Community Church for the better part of a decade. It's no trouble to pick up you, too."

"Still, I appreciate it," Lily told her. "I wouldn't have gone on my own."

"I assumed as much," Coraline said. "The committee members agreed not to press the newcomers to join any group in town until you'd had a chance to settle in and establish yourselves, but I thought you might appreciate getting out."

"Very much," Lily told her.

The three women chatted about that and the flower arrangements that Lily had put together for the new businesses as they drove to the church. Coraline raised her eyebrows at the idea of using such things as old bread boxes, percolators and rusty pipes as vases, but Ann bragged about Lily's artistic eye. Privately Lily basked in the praise.

They parked next to the front walk. Lily got out while Coraline gathered her Bible and handbag. The old white clapboard church looked like something from another era, with its diamond-shaped window above a tiny vestibule and a stately steeple towering over the sanctuary. A newer section of the building branched off at the back, giving the building a T shape. Lily could imagine those original Bronsons climbing the steps to the vestibule as the bell rang from the steeple, the ladies in long draped skirts, the gentlemen in their frock coats. Miss Ann got out on her side and started forward, but Lily felt rooted to the graveled parking lot until Coraline reached back and linked arms with her.

"Come along. And smile. No one's going to bite you."

Lily laughed, her shell of uncertainty cracking. Her feet barely touched the sidewalk before the townsfolk descended. Coraline stayed close, making brief introductions and forging ahead toward the steps. Lily nodded and replied softly to every greeting, smiling all the while and letting Coraline tow her toward the building. Just as they reached the steps up to the narrow double vestibule doors, Ginny Bronson rounded the corner of the building with her granddaughter. Isabella broke into a run, a sheaf of papers fluttering in her hands.

"Lily! Grandma, Lily's here. Look what I got for you, Lily."

Lily pulled free of Coraline and stooped to catch the child, going almost to one knee. "Hi! I didn't know I'd see you here."

"You've saved me a side trip," Ginny said, shielding her eyes from the morning sun with an upraised hand.

The girl thrust the papers at Lily, exclaiming, "I did all the flowers for you. See!"

"She hasn't let them out of her sight all morning," Ginny explained.

Lily took the papers, straightened them as best she could and began sorting through them. "Why, Isabella, did you color all of these?"

"Uh-huh, and I stayed in all the lines."

"You did. How pretty."

Isabella pulled one free and held it up. "This one's my favorite!" She had colored each petal of a sunflower a different shade, everything from yellow to magenta.

"A rainbow flower," Lily said. "Very creative." Isabella beamed.

"I drawed one," she reported, "but Daddy says it looks more like a fireworks than a flower. What do you think?"

"A lot of the fireworks the other night looked like flowers," Lily noted, going through the papers to find one that had been hand-drawn.

Lily caught a look passing between Coraline and Ginny. She assumed that the latter had just confirmed that Lily had spent the Fourth of July with the Bronson family. Lily wished that she could tell them not to read too much into that. Instead she concentrated on Isabella.

"Oh, this is definitely a flower," Lily declared. Isabella's little chest puffed up. Lily neatened the papers and held them carefully against her heart. "Thank you. What a perfect present."

Isabella literally preened. "You're welcome."

Ginny Bronson shared another look with Coraline then pressed a hand to her granddaughter's back. "We'd best get inside now. Don't want to be late."

They went off to climb the steps and disappear through the double doors into the tiny vestibule of the church. Lily looked down thoughtfully at the stack of papers in her hands then abruptly smiled as an idea came to her.

"Did you ever pray then suddenly get an answer?"

"Oh, yes," Coraline told her. "I might be looking at a living, breathing answer to prayer at this very moment."

Lily took a deep breath. "You're talking about the town, of course."

Coraline smiled gently. "Yes. That and other things."

Before Lily could ask her to explain that, Coraline joined Ann, and the two women climbed the steps to enter the vestibule. Lily carefully tucked Isabella's crayon-colored pictures into her Bible and followed.

A percolator. Tate shook his head in wonder. She'd used a rusty old percolator, turned it on its side and had it spilling flowers, along with coffee grounds, so artistically that people stood around gaping at it. Josh Smith had joked that people were too busy staring at Lily's flower arrangement to buy coffee, but judging by the line at the counter, that wasn't strictly true. Still, it had drawn a crowd.

Tate had forced himself to stop in the Cozy Cup Café first on that Grand Opening Monday, reasoning that his impulse to go charging over to the floral shop could not bode well for anyone, especially after Isabella had harangued him about checking on Lily all weekend. After seeing Lily's creation on display at the coffee shop, however, he hadn't been able to make himself go inside the bakery, which was the logical next stop. Though gratified by the line trailing out the front door, he had paused only long enough to look through the window.

When the crowd had parted, he'd caught a glimpse of the bread box Lily had shown him the

other day. Painted white and trimmed in pink, it
disgorged a froth of pastel blossoms sparkling with
some sort of glitter. The arrangement looked good
enough to eat, and people kept touching the flowers to see if they were real.

Amazed at the inventiveness of the town's young
florist, Tate avoided two women on the sidewalk—
one carrying long-stemmed carnations and another
a small arrangement in a ceramic baby shoe—on his
way to Love in Bloom. No line snaked out the front
door of the flower shop, but the place was jammed,
as Tate discovered the instant that he opened the
door.

Lily looked up with a ready smile from rearranging the glass display shelves, but the blue eyes behind her glasses showed signs of strain. Before Tate
could greet her, a woman holding a squat burgundy
vase asked Lily a question. The pair then turned
and walked toward the humidifier to pick out flowers. Tate took the opportunity to look around the
shop. She had achieved a charming mix of innocence and sophistication with her décor. At first he
couldn't imagine how she had done it, but then he
looked closer.

Astonished, he stepped up to the shelves she had
been rearranging and studied them in detail. Isabella's colored sheets peeked out at him from amidst
figurines and vases filled with flowers both real and
silk. Lily had trimmed the images, encased them
in glass and framed them with ribbon color-coded

to the picture and the display. Isabella would be thrilled. *He* was thrilled and not a little proud of both Lily and his daughter.

As he looked around the shop, the bell above the door continually rang, with people coming and going. The cash register rang quite often, too, Tate noticed. He also noticed that Lily seemed frazzled already. Deciding he'd been patient enough, Tate made his way to her and shoved his as yet untouched iced coffee into her hands.

"You look like you could use this. They're giving them away over at the Cozy Cup, but I prefer my coffee hot and black, even in the middle of July."

Lily took the light brown cup into her finely boned hand and sipped at the contents. She looked very pretty in a long soft yellow top with elbow-length sleeves and matching pants. The slashed neck of the top had been embroidered with purple flowers and green ivy. She had caught her long hair in a loose ponytail below her left ear. Tate tried to remember if he had seen those small gold hoop earrings carved with ivy leaves before, but he kept getting distracted by the delicacy of her earlobes.

"You look great," he heard himself say. Glancing away, he tried to bury that compliment with another. "The shop looks wonderful. Isabella will be so proud."

"She gave me exactly what I needed," Lily told him.

As if summoned by the mention of her name,

his daughter pushed through the door just then, the bell jangling over her little head. Her grandmother followed, along with Gracie Wilson. Isabella had hung on Gracie for a while, until she'd realized that Gracie had no more interest in Tate than he had in her. Now that Gracie was engaged to marry Trent Morgan, they could greet each other as easy friends again.

"Hey, Tate."

"Gracie, good to see you. Isabella, look." Tate pointed to one of her crayon creations. Lily took it off the shelf and showed it to her then put it back.

"Makes a pretty display, don't you think?"

Isabella let out a shriek and threw herself at Lily, somehow dodging an elderly couple picking through a display of ivies in miniature pots. Lily quickly passed the coffee back to Tate and scooped up his daughter. Carrying her around the room, she pointed out each coloring. His mom, meanwhile, took Gracie around. Presently Gracie and his mother approached Lily and Isabella, who seemed to be trying to squeeze Lily's head from her body with one of her "power hugs."

Ginny plucked her granddaughter from Lily's arms, declaring, "Lily and Gracie need to discuss business now."

Gracie bluntly exclaimed, "I want you to do the flowers for my wedding at the end of August."

Lily beamed. "Lovely." She waved a hand at a small glass-topped table and a pair of delicate chairs tucked into a corner. "Let me show you my design catalog."

"I want to keep it simple," Gracie said, hurrying over to seat herself.

Lily followed. Remaining on her feet, she pulled a thick binder forward and flipped it open. "Let me know when you see something you like."

Tate thought grumpily that she might at least have looked in his direction before letting herself get caught up with Gracie's wedding plans. Frowning, he took a long drink of the cold coffee, only to hear his mother ask, "Isn't that Lily's?"

"What?" he asked. Ginny looked pointedly at the cup in his hand. "Oh. No, it's mine, actually."

Ginny lifted her eyebrows but said only, "I promised Isabella a treat, so we're going to get in line at the bakery next door. Care to join us?"

"Uh, I think I'll mosey on down the street." He wanted to see the arrangements that Lily had done for the other businesses.

"Will you be home for lunch?" Ginny asked.

Tate made a doubtful face. "I expect I'd better stay in town. The ladies on the committee have put together some sort of covered dish thing for lunch, I think. Don't count on seeing me again until after the reception this evening." It occurred to him that he ought to be at Lily's side during the reception. He was, after all, her official committee contact and host.

"In that case Isabella can stay at our house tonight," Ginny offered, but he automatically shook his head.

"I'll just pick her up later."

Ginny sighed. "All right, son. Whatever you say."

"Thanks, Mom." He kissed her cheek then Isabella's. "Behave yourself, sprite."

"Yes, Daddy."

Ginny carried her out of the shop, Isabella babbling about her pictures and wanting to see the book and pet shops. Tate wanted to see those shops, too, but probably not for the same reasons as his daughter. He dithered a moment longer, watching Lily as she guided Gracie through the photo album and kept an eye on the other customers in the store. Lily needed help. Hopefully she would soon need someone permanent. He had a list, drawn up by the committee, of local people with related skills, but now was not the time to bring up that subject. He would save that for later.

Finding a strange kind of comfort in that thought, he went out to see what other works of art his florist from Boston had wrought. Well, not *his*. Lily was Bygones' florist. If he was feeling a tad possessive, it was only because he was her SOS contact. And a complete fool.

Chapter Six

Exhausted but pleased, Lily locked the door of the shop and crossed the street beneath the Grand Opening banner. Miss Mars waited for her on the sidewalk in front of the insurance agency, which seemed to have given away a sizable number of small calendars and ink pens that day. Miss Mars had told her that the agency, a long-established business, was owned by a group in Manhattan, Kansas, and managed by a local couple.

"The day is a success!" Miss Mars announced, waving one of the hankies she had given away by the dozens. They walked at Miss Mars's speed toward the Community Room.

"Where did they all come from?" Lily asked, happily relieved.

At one point that afternoon, Main Street had actually enjoyed such a traffic jam that the chief of police himself had come out to direct parking into the school lot behind the Cozy Cup Café.

Miss Mars divulged that the committee had purchased advertisements in local newspapers throughout the county and as far away as Junction City and Manhattan. "People kept asking where they could get lunch. We should have chosen a restaurant as one of the new businesses," she opined, "but we were afraid the town wouldn't be able to support a full-service restaurant again long-term."

"The Everything must have done good business today," Lily said. "I told half a dozen people how to find it."

"The Dills will be thrilled, I expect."

They reached the Community Room, and Lily pushed open the door, holding it for Miss Mars then following her inside. They stepped into a hum of ongoing conversations. A table of refreshments had been set up, and several rows of folding chairs ringed the plain white room, but as many people stood as sat. Tate lifted an arm, gesturing them toward two chairs that he had saved. As they made their way through the throng, Lily picked up snippets.

"Yeah, sure, lots of folks came in, but it was just one day. How you going to get 'em back?"

"Pets. How many pets can you buy in a month, now, I ask you?"

"You just get one birthday a year. In our house that's four birthday cakes for the whole year. And most folks hereabouts just bake their own, don't you think?"

"Flowers grow right out in the front yard," Lily heard one man say, "and my wife pays ten bucks for carnations. I'll be putting a stop to that, let me tell you."

The good feeling that Lily had enjoyed earlier began to fade, then Tate pointed to a table against the wall.

"What do you think?"

Someone had brought in all of the arrangements she'd done for the other shops and lined them up on the table for display. "Oh, look. That's sweet."

"That's nuts is what that is," said an angry voice behind her.

Tate frowned, and Lily spun to face her detractor.

"That's uncalled for, Brian."

"Uncalled for?" the man demanded. "I'll tell you what's uncalled for. Girly cakes and fancy flowers, that's what's uncalled for! Why do people need that stuff? What good is it when their cars break down?"

"Brian, I know you're disappointed that the committee didn't choose to bring in a mechanic's shop, but the investment required to do that was just too high."

"So you go for *frills?* Come on, Tate. It's a dumb waste of funds."

"Dumb?" Tate echoed. "Have you even looked at what Lily's done? It's nothing short of genius! And you, Brian Montclair, are a sore loser. You pushed for what you wanted, you didn't get it and now you're behaving like a sullen child. The committee didn't make its decisions lightly. We have good reasons for what we've done, and I think we chose well when it comes to our new business owners."

"We'll see, won't we?" Brian Montclair returned darkly before turning to disappear into the crowd.

Lily sighed. "And I thought the day had gone so well."

"It has gone well," Tate insisted. "I'll admit, it's just one day, and no one knows what the future holds, but today, at least, has exceeded my personal expectations."

"Hear, hear," Miss Mars agreed. "A good start, I say."

"Let's pray that it continues," Lily murmured. "Now, the two of you save our seats while I get us some refreshments."

"I can do that," Tate volunteered, but Lily shook her head.

"No, I want to."

"Well, if you're sure."

"Yes, thank you."

She went off to fetch punch, cookies and the most beautiful petit fours she'd ever seen. Mostly, though, she went so she could stand in line and hug to herself something that Tate had said to Brian Montclair.

Have you even looked at what Lily's done? It's nothing short of genius.

Genius.

Her.

She didn't think she'd felt so complimented in her

life, not even when Mayor Langston had stopped her to rave about her floral designs.

Short and solid, with thinning gray hair, the mayor was a man in his late fifties or thereabout. He carried a cane hooked over his right forearm and a clear plastic plate of goodies in his left hand. Lily saw that the tips of two of his fingers were missing. "Mayor," as he told her to call him, mentioned that his wife, Helen, appreciated Lily buying canned shrimp down at their grocery. While Lily was trying to digest this stunning information and picture in her mind how tall lean Helen and squat, at-least-a-decade-older Mayor Langston had come together as a couple, a pair of aging flower children strolled up.

They could be none other than the Dills. He, of the chest-length graying beard, wore a leather vest over a tie-dyed T-shirt and bell-bottom jeans cinched in with a beaded belt. She wore a gathered skirt, a Hawaiian shirt belted with a scarf, and a lei. Her ponytail hung to her ample hips. Both wore sandals and sported tattoos on their forearms and necks. Elwood nodded and grinned at her, waving a petit four iced in pink fondant and decorated with miniature violets.

"You ladies at the bakery, flower shop and bookstore really class up the joint," he declared.

His wife nodded, and the pair shuffled off to spread their cheer and enjoy their cakes elsewhere. Someone chuckled behind her.

"Bygones doesn't lack for local color, does it?"

Lily turned to offer an uncertain smile, recognizing Josh Smith, proprietor of the Cozy Cup Café. "Takes all kinds, I suppose."

"It certainly does." Tall, with auburn hair and green eyes, he looked to be about her age. "I wanted to tell you that your flower arrangement received many complimentary comments today."

"Thanks. I heard lots of good things about your coffee, too. I personally love it."

He inclined his head. "Thank you. Anyone mention the internet café?"

Lily smiled wanly and tried to think of something positive to say. She had heard lots of comment, but most of them had sounded confused. "The kids are really excited about it."

Josh chuckled. "We're going to offer some LAN competitions later on."

"Online group games, you mean."

"Exactly."

"That's cool."

"Ought to give them something to do besides sit in front of The Everything."

Lily took a deep breath and asked, "You're optimistic then? About the town's chances of making this all work, I mean. Because I'm hearing some negative comments."

Josh glanced around, joking, "Maybe they just need more coffee."

That wasn't quite the reassurance for which she'd

been hoping, but she smiled and helped herself to the lovely desserts on offer. When she turned, her hands full, Tate caught her eye by holding up two glasses of punch to let her know that he'd taken care of that end of things. Lily felt her heart warm.

Tate appreciated her design acumen. That was something she'd hold close for a long time to come. She just had to remember that they were friends, nothing more, and that the important thing was to make the shop a success, for the sake of the town, as well as her own pocketbook. As if to underscore that, Mayor Langston walked to the center of the room, banged his cane on the wood floor and called for quiet just as Lily got back to her seat. Eventually the room hushed.

The mayor then leaned upon his cane and proceeded to thank everyone for coming out to make the Heart of Main Street Grand Opening a success. This brought applause. The mayor then asked all the newcomers to rise, and he introduced them one by one, beginning with Chase Rollins, proprietor of the Fluff & Stuff pet store. Quite tall, with black hair and brown eyes, Chase seemed tense to Lily, but she'd watched him handle tiny gerbils and hamsters with exquisite tenderness. He stood and nodded before promptly seating himself again.

Patrick Fogerty of The Fixer-Upper came next. In his midthirties and standing even taller than Rollins, Fogerty was very good-looking, a real tall-dark-and-handsome type. On the quiet side, he managed to exude an affability that made Lily feel comfortable despite her tendency to be tongue-tied around such men.

Allison True, of the Happy Endings Bookstore, was a native of Bygones but had apparently been gone for many years. A pretty brunette a couple years younger than Lily, Allison seemed a bit of a mystery. She'd done an outstanding job with her shop, and Lily hoped they would become friends over time.

When Lily's turn came, she found herself blushing with the praise heaped upon her for her imaginative flower arrangements. While pleasant to hear such compliments, it was also difficult to take being the center of attention. She kept trying to sit down, and Tate kept pushing her back up, until finally Melissa Sweeney's turn came and Lily could sit in peace.

A real sweetheart and as tall as Lily, but with considerably more curve, Melissa had lovely red hair, gorgeous green eyes and enough energy for ten women. She would need it. A bakery was a workhouse, especially when one was as detail-oriented as Melissa seemed to be.

Last came Josh Smith with his quiet wit and self-deprecating smile. Laidback and easygoing, Josh always seemed in need of a caffeine jolt. Perhaps that lay behind his choice of business.

After introducing the newcomers, Mayor Langston introduced the other Save Our Streets Committee members. Lily couldn't help being glad that she had drawn Tate as her official committee contact and host. He didn't exactly make her feel comfortable—the opposite, in fact—but he drew her in a way that she couldn't quite describe. She didn't feel like such an outsider with Tate. When he was around, she felt that things were as they should be, that all would work out well. Even given her tendency to form unwise attachments to men with whom she worked, she wouldn't have traded Tate for anyone else on the committee, not even Coraline or Miss Mars. Besides, knowing that she and Tate couldn't ever be more than friends would surely curb any inclination she might have to form a crush on him. Surely.

The mayor commended the committee for its many hours of hard work and explained that they had been through literally hundreds of applications for each of the half dozen grants ultimately approved. He talked about the business plans submitted and the great jobs done by the newcomers and committee members alike. In the end he pronounced the Grand Opening a success and urged the town to support the new businesses at every opportunity, saying that if these first six were successful, they could "build on this base." He invited everyone to remain as long as the food and drink lasted, but just as he seemed about to yield the floor, Whitney Leigh, the reporter from the *Bygones Gazette,* all but leaped into the opening. The neat young blonde with the severe bun and glasses wielded a tiny voice recorder as if it were a weapon.

"Mayor," she cried in a challenging voice, "on behalf of the citizens of the city of Bygones, I demand to know who the mystery benefactor is behind the grants that brought these businesses to town."

Mayor Langston gripped his cane, sighing. "Whitney, I've told you and told you. I don't have any idea who our anonymous benefactor is. Hence, the words *anonymous* and *mystery*."

Whitney edged closer, holding out her recorder. "Sir," she pressed, "aren't you concerned about this individual's possible ulterior motives?"

Whispers instantly sprang up in various corners around the room.

"What possible ulterior motives?" the mayor asked. "He or she makes funds available, no strings attached."

"That's not true," Whitney insisted. "There is the two-year minimum residency requirement, the good faith effort requirement, the matching funds on deposit, the expectation that locals be hired, the grant repayment in case the aforementioned terms aren't met…"

"That's on the grant receivers, not the town," the mayor pointed out.

With her free hand Whitney smoothed the waistband of her slender knee-length skirt where it met her severely tailored blouse. "But this person now owns half of downtown."

"So? It's half of downtown that was in receivership and going to ruin."

"I still say we should know who we're doing business with," Whitney proclaimed, lifting her chin. "And that's the *Gazette's* official position."

"I know. I read your editorials," the mayor returned, "and I still say we shouldn't look a gift horse in the mouth." With that, he turned away, shaking his head.

"Girl's right," someone near Lily murmured. "We're heading for trouble."

"Whole thing's a pipe dream anyhow," someone else groused. "Bound to fail."

Lily instinctively turned to Tate for reassurance. "That's not true, is it? Our businesses can succeed in Bygones, can't they?"

Tate shrugged, his lips compressed in a flat line. "There are no guarantees, Lily. We've made a good start, but…"

"Now, now," Coraline said, appearing at Tate's elbow, "none of that. So far so good, I say, and if we continue to work hard and pray for success, I see no reason for God to withdraw His favor."

Tate's face tightened. The softness in his eyes hardened to a cold brown glitter. It was as if a wall of ice suddenly encased him.

"You do that, ma'am," he said with excruciating politeness. "I'm just not one to count on God's favor." He looked to Lily then, saying, "I'll be around with that list of prospective employees.

Now, if you'll excuse me…" He gave a nod, stepped back and simply walked away, wending through the crowd to the door.

Lily stared after him, confused and disappointed. Beside her, Coraline sighed.

"Will that boy never get over his anger at God over Eve's death?"

"What?" Lily asked, stunned. "But that's so sad."

"Oh, don't worry," Coraline told her, patting her hand, "not for your own prospects, anyway. You'll do well here. Business will soon bloom at your lovely little florist's shop. I feel sure of it."

Lily tried to smile, but she couldn't help noticing that Coraline had left Tate out of her assurances about Lily's "prospects." Just as she should. Why then did it rankle so?

Rolling the paper containing the list of prospective employees in his hand, Tate tapped the brim of his straw hat with it. Part of his official duty as Lily's committee contact was to see to it that she hired someone local to staff her shop. He hadn't realized when the list was drawn up that they were dealing with such an artistic soul. He'd thought of a florist as a glorified gardener, someone who puttered around with flowers and ribbons. How was he to know that she could create works of art with those things?

Aware of his appearance as he hadn't been before, Tate smoothed the front of his clean white shirt and straightened the buckle of his belt before reaching for the handle on the door of the shop. That was when he realized Lily already had a caller. He recognized the rotund, bewigged, loudly dressed fortyish gentleman on sight.

Entering the building, he heard Dale Eversleigh say, "I think we'll start with a standing order for a fresh arrangement once a month."

"That's wonderful," Lily said, scribbling on an order pad. She looked up long enough to greet Tate. "Hi. Be with you in a minute."

"No problem."

Smiling, she went back to business. "And what were you thinking of in terms of size and color?"

"Nothing too large," Dale told her, ignoring the new arrival. "Something suitable for our receptionist's desk, seasonal colors."

While Lily and Dale hashed out the details, Tate occupied himself by studying the display shelves. She'd replaced a good bit of inventory; Tate assumed that meant she'd made many sales during their big Grand Opening.

"I think it would be a good idea if we could have a copy of your catalog to keep at the funeral home," Dale said. "That way we could show it to our clients there, perhaps even save them an unnecessary stop during their time of bereavement."

"That could work," Lily said hesitantly. "Um, but were you thinking of adding a surcharge for the service?"

Tate glanced over to see how Eversleigh took that. The corpulent undertaker shook his head, his obvious blond wig stiff and unresponsive. Capturing Lily's hand, he patted it, pinky ring flashing. Tate folded his arms, wondering if Dale wasn't being just a bit too familiar. Lily was not a client, after all.

"I wouldn't dream of it," Dale said in a deep, velvety voice.

Tate told himself that Dale spoke like that purely out of habit, then he caught himself thinking, *That had better be the case.* Shaken by the unexpected surge of possessiveness, Tate stiffened.

Lily smiled at Dale. "I'll have a copy of my catalog for you by Friday then."

"Excellent." Dale patted her hand again. "I'll pick it up on Saturday, shall I?"

"That's fine," Lily said distractedly, removing her hand from Dale's in order to make notes on her pad.

Tate relaxed a bit—until Dale suddenly asked Lily, "Do you play golf?"

Tate's jaw dropped. Why, the old dog! Everyone knew that Dale Eversleigh had a penchant for the ladies and a passion for golf, but he was much too old for Lily. And to make a play for her with Tate standing right there! Frowning, Tate parked his hands at his belt, the list paper crinkling. Eversleigh glanced over his shoulder as if only then recalling that he wasn't alone in the shop with Lily.

"Ah, no," she said, after a start of surprise. "I—I've never had any interest in golf."

Dale pursed his lips. "Pity." He reached into the pocket of his plaid pants to jingle his keys. "Very well. See you on Saturday then. Good morning."

"Good morning, Mr. Eversleigh," Lily said, "and thank you."

"My pleasure." He nodded to Lily, then to Tate, and went out.

"What a nice man," Lily murmured as the door closed behind him.

"Lily!" Tate erupted. "Dale Eversleigh was hitting on you."

"What?" She laughed and shook her head. "Oh, no, I'm sure he was just inviting me to join the golf club or—"

"There is no golf club. Trust me on this. Dale Eversleigh considers himself Bygones's gift to women. He was hitting on you."

Lily pointed out the door through which Eversleigh had so recently passed. "He… But he's so…" Suddenly she clapped her hands over her lower face. A snort was quickly followed by giggles and several hard swallows and, finally, a deep breath, after which she lowered her hands. "I, um, have never before seen an undertaker d-dress in yellow-and-green plaid."

Tickled, Tate forced a sober manner. "Well, the shirt was yellow-and-green. Technically, the pants were yellow, green *and orange*."

Her lips wiggled. She straightened them and

squared her shoulders. "Is he actually an undertaker? Not a bereavement counselor o-or casket salesman?"

"Third-generation mortician," Tate confirmed evenly. "All the Eversleighs are certified undertakers, three brothers, three funeral homes around the county."

Her blue eyes grew quite large behind the lenses of her glasses. "Are the other two Eversleighs like him?"

Tate shook his head thoughtfully. "Now that you mention it, no. Dale is one of a kind. The other two are more staid, I guess you'd say, and both married."

She shrugged so eloquently that Tate grinned, feeling quite generous all of a sudden.

"All kidding aside, Dale's harmless and a decent guy. He's given plenty of folks around here a break when they couldn't afford his services. I doubt he even thought of applying a surcharge for letting people order your flowers from the funeral home."

"That's good to know," Lily said, smiling. "I'll keep that in mind in the future."

"Just don't play golf with him," Tate warned good-naturedly.

Lily chuckled. "No, I wouldn't, even if he were interested in me, which I doubt."

Tate, who for some reason couldn't seem to leave well enough alone, scoffed at that. "He's interested."

Lily ducked her head, pushing up her glasses at the same time, and said, "Not likely. I'm not the sort men notice. If I were, I'd have had at least one real boyfriend by now. Don't you think?"

For the second time in the space of a quarter-hour, Tate felt his jaw drop. She could not be serious. How did a woman like her get to be twenty-seven years of age without some guy seeing how special and lovely and talented she was? Dale had seen it, and Tate felt certain that others around town had seen it, too. Sure, she was a bit reticent, but her sweetness more than made up for that. Isabella adored her.

What was he thinking? Isabella would adore any woman who gave her the time of day, any woman of an age to be her... The word *mother* made him step back.

Lily tried to smile, but her gaze did not meet his and the apples of her cheeks glowed a pronounced shade of pink. "E-excuse me, b-but I have some... things to do."

"Right," Tate muttered, remembering the paper curled inside his fist. "I, uh, brought over the list of people the committee recommends." He spread the paper on the counter. "Everyone listed here is anxious to work."

"I understand."

He left the paper on the counter and rubbed his hands together lightly. "I'll leave you to it, then." He all but ran from the shop and leaped into the truck.

What was wrong with him, anyway? He had no business getting upset by the likes of Dale Eversleigh. What did he care if Lily played golf with

Dale? Not that she was going to. A fact about which he had no business being relieved.

He had done his duty, and now, for all intents and purposes, he was done. Lily would hire someone from Bygones to help in her shop, the first person on the list, most likely, and that would be that.

Kenneth Wilbur would serve her well. Nearing forty with a teenage son and a mother suffering from early-onset Alzheimer's, Kenneth had managed to keep body and soul together by eating out of his impressive garden and doing odd jobs around town. He was scruffy and a bit rough around the edges, but Kenneth had a true affinity for anything that grew out of the ground. Lily would surely see that and hire him. With Kenneth Wilbur around to take care of things, Tate could essentially wash his hands of Lily.

And anytime now, he was going to be relieved about *that*.

Chapter Seven

It was a tough decision. Lily had not expected hiring someone to be so tough. In Boston an employer advertised, collected résumés, interviewed prospects and chose the person who seemed to be the best fit for the position. Here in Bygones, however, everyone desperately needed the income and no one was a great fit for the job. Lily was so terrified of making a mistake that she thought about calling Tate to ask his advice. In the end she called Coraline, who came and prayed with her.

"Now, don't worry," Coraline told her. "You'll do fine. Trust God to show you the right person for the job."

"I just feel so bad for those I can't hire."

"Of course you do, but God will provide. Tate can help you notify those whom you can't hire." Knowing that helped a little.

Lily went to bed confident that she would soon have answers. Sure enough, she woke the next day with a specific person in mind. She realized at once that she'd been leaning that way all along, and when she really thought about why, her reasons crystallized. She dressed, ate breakfast and went downstairs to open the shop. Then she called Sherie Taylor and let her know that she could start work right away. Sherie was thrilled. The others, naturally, would not be, but Lily depended on Tate to help her notify them that they had not been chosen.

When she called his cell phone, it went to voice mail, so she left a message, letting him know that she had hired Sherie. She'd hardly ended the call before Sherie showed up, eager to begin work. Lily liked her enthusiasm.

Of average height and a bit pudgy, with short, curly, light brown hair and lively green eyes, Sherie was the divorced mom of twin boys, ten years of age. She had moved in with her parents and made do with child support and unemployment since the plant had closed, but her good nature and sunny smile had not suffered. She had studied design in college but never finished the degree and expressed a true interest in learning all the elements of flower arranging and corsage making. Of everyone Lily had interviewed, Sherie had expressed the most interest in both the technique and the art of floral design. Plus, she just seemed like a good fit personality-wise.

Lily imagined how pleased Tate would be.

She imagined, too, that he had been just a tiny

bit jealous when Dale Eversleigh had held her hand and asked her if she liked to play golf. That was all it was, of course, imagination, nothing more than a dream. That was what Lily had done most of her life, after all, dream of one guy or another, without ever speaking up or taking a single step to draw or fix the interest of anyone who attracted her. She was good at imagining and dreaming. Well, she was done with that. All it had ever done was lead her into dissatisfaction and heartbreak.

For the first time she decided that she ought to ask God how to get good at *doing*. She hadn't come to Bygones to repeat the mistakes of her past; she had come to start a business, to make a new home and a new life. It was time to dig down deep inside herself and make things happen. She wasn't afraid of hard work. She could be who she was, just as God had made her, and still make new friends and learn a new way of living.

Bygones wasn't Boston. Things weren't as easy or convenient here, but this was where God had planted her, and she was determined to grow and blossom. She didn't need some man for that. All this new life needed was a lot of work, some hope and a little faith on her part. She could manage that. She *would* manage that, and her reward would be a sense of accomplishment and satisfaction.

Resolute, she put Tate Bronson out of mind and concentrated on business. Bookkeeping had to be set up now that she had a couple of regular accounts.

Assigning Sherie to watch the shop, she went into the office and did her best to figure out the accounting software. Two hours later she decided that she'd better take a break before she took a hammer to the computer.

"How's it coming?" Sherie asked.

"It isn't. I think I have everything entered, but it won't save. I don't know what I'm doing wrong."

"You haven't set up the file," Sherie said matter-of-factly. "Why don't you let me set it up for you?"

"Truly? You can set up accounts receivable?" Lily grasped Sherie by both arms and shook her slightly. "Please tell me you can set up accounts receivable."

Sherie chuckled. "I worked in accounting at Randall's. I think I can set up the computer books without much trouble."

Lily turned her face upward and closed her eyes. "Thank You, God."

"Amen to that," Sherie said. "Now, I'll be in the office if you need me."

"I need you in the office is where I need you," Lily quipped as the other woman headed down the hall. The bell over the door tinkled merrily, and Lily turned, beaming, to find Tate, frowning, on the other side of her counter, his cap in his hand, the bill folded almost double. She wished her heart would not leap every time she saw him.

"Hello."

"Hello."

He made a point of watching Sherie until she

disappeared into the small office that opened off the short narrow hallway behind Lily. Then his gaze switched to Lily's face.

"Really?" he hissed quietly. "Sherie Taylor was your choice?"

Stung, Lily drew back. "What's wrong with Sherie?"

"Nothing's *wrong* with Sherie, but she has her parents to help her, while Kenneth Wilbur is taking care of a parent, not to mention a teenage son, with no help whatsoever."

Blinking, Lily matched his frown with one of her own. "What are you getting at?"

"I thought you'd hire Kenneth."

"You mean, you thought I *should* hire Kenneth."

"All right. I thought, I *think,* you should hire Kenneth."

"How was I to know that?" Lily whispered. "You didn't say so."

"I thought you'd figure it out when you interviewed him," Tate said, tight-lipped.

Lily walked around the counter, caught Tate by the arm and drew him into the front corner of the shop.

"All I learned from Kenneth Wilbur's interview," she said softly, "was that he has no interest in learning design, prefers not to wait on customers and thinks I should be selling more potted plants than cut flowers. Sherie, on the other hand, understands the elements of design, wants to work with the flowers, likes to interact with customers and is back there setting up my accounts receivable right now." She folded her arms. "Given that, which one would you choose if you were me?"

Tate slapped his hat against his thigh. "All I know is that Kenneth needs a break."

"I'm going to be buying herbs and other potted plants from him," Lily revealed in a normal tone.

"That's not enough to keep the wolf from the door," Tate muttered.

Just then the bell jingled again. Lily craned her neck to look around Tate.

"Pastor Garman. Mrs. Garman. How nice to see you. Come in."

Tate stepped aside, nodding, so Lily could move back behind the counter. Wendy Garman, a little wren of a woman well into her sixties, with gray-brown helmet-hair and enormous eyeglasses, greeted Tate by name then laid a sheet of paper on the counter.

"Hugh and I thought it would be a good idea to make a sign-up chart for altar flowers," she told Lily.

The pastor, a tall slender man, bald except for a fringe of fading reddish-brown hair, bushy eyebrows and a prodigious mustache, spoke up then. "We hope that our church members will volunteer to provide flower arrangements to decorate the altar and commemorate dates and occasions special to them, such as birthdays and anniversaries. To get the ball rolling, Wendy and I are going to sign up to provide flowers on the Sunday nearest to our own birthdays."

"What a lovely idea," Lily said. "We should probably set a dollar limit so no one will feel obligated to spend too much."

Mrs. Garman seemed relieved by that. Coraline had told Lily that Hugh had been ready to retire when the Randall plant closed, but the church had lost so many members so quickly that they soon could not afford to pay a minister's salary. Hugh had volunteered to stay on at a quarter of his original pay, take his Social Security and consider himself semiretired. Wendy took over the position of church secretary in return for continued residence in the church parsonage, where the Garmans kept "office hours." Their teenage grandson, whose widowed father was a missionary in Turkey, lived there with them.

"A dollar limit seems like a good plan," Wendy agreed. "Perhaps we can take a special collection for flower arrangements at Christmas and Easter."

"I'm sure we can come up with something special but not too expensive for those occasions," Lily told her, checking over their calendar.

As she ran her eyes over the chart, she saw that the Garmans had filled in members' birthdays and anniversaries. When she saw Isabella's birthday on the next to the last Sunday of the month, she instantly looked to Tate, making what seemed a natural assumption.

"I guess you'll be wanting to sign up to provide altar flowers for the twenty-first."

Tate's face turned to stone. Too late, Lily recalled that Isabella's birthday was also the anniversary of the death of Tate's wife.

The pastor and his wife exchanged a glance then went on talking as if Lily had not just committed a terrible faux pas, saying that they would display their copy of the sign-up calendar in the vestibule of the church and check it weekly, then keep Lily apprised of who might be calling her to order. They stiltedly discussed a few more details before the Garmans prepared to take their leave.

"We hope to see you again this coming Sunday."

"Thank you," she managed softly. "I'll be there."

Smiling and nodding, they moved to leave. Pastor Garman held the door for his wife then started through himself, pausing at the last moment to speak to Tate.

"It was good to see you, Tate. You've been missed."

For a moment Lily thought Tate would not respond, but then he turned and nodded.

"Take care of yourselves."

The bell jingled above the door as it closed on the Garmans. Lily stepped out from behind the counter to move swiftly to stand before Tate.

"I'm so sorry. What I said earlier was thought-less and presumptuous."

He squeezed his eyes closed as if pained. For an instant she felt torn between the impulse to run and hide and the need to somehow comfort him. The latter won out; it wasn't even really much of a con-test. Without giving herself time to think too much, she stepped up and wrapped her arms around him. This was her *acting,* just as she'd asked God to help her do. She would not be too reticent to comfort a friend just because he was a man whom she found attractive, especially not when she had hurt him.

Seconds ticked by as his hands drifted up to set-tle at her waist and his head bowed.

"It's not your fault," he whispered.

She shook her head, feeling her hair ripple across her back and shoulders. "I didn't think before I spoke. I just assumed—"

"Shhh." He inched closer, saying, "It's under-standable, and of course I celebrate my daughter's birthday, but you're sweet to worry about my feel-ings."

Smiling, she looked up—straight into his warm brown eyes. And, oh, my, those dimples. She didn't know who moved, if she did or he did, but some-how their lips met.

Lightly, gently. It might have been a kiss between friends, a simple, almost meaningless gesture, but it wasn't. The earth did not move. Worlds did not collide. Reality did not shatter. Yet, in that soft, sweet, ephemeral instant, everything changed.

What had not been before suddenly was, and Lily thought with shuddering wonder, *I did this. I set this in motion when I put my arms around him.*

After a moment Tate stepped back. Lily hadn't decided where to look or what to say when the bell tinkled over the door. She whirled around to find Coraline there.

"Hello, you two," she said, tilting her head to one side.

Lily smiled brightly, perhaps too brightly, and moved back behind the counter. "H-hi. How are you today?"

"Well. Thank you." Coraline carefully moved forward and placed her pocketbook on the counter as if negotiating a tricky maneuver. "I'd like to pick up something to cheer a friend who's feeling poorly."

"Aw, th-that's sweet," Lily stammered.

Tate jerked forward as if she'd poked him. Lily felt like biting her tongue. She would have to remind him that he'd described her as "sweet"—just before they'd kissed.

"I'll be going now," he said quickly, "since you've already hired someone."

"I'm sorry about Mr. Wilbur," she told Tate, fighting the impulse to follow him to the door.

"What about Kenneth?" Coraline wanted to know, sounding concerned.

Tate waved a hand. "Uh, Lily's going to buy some potted plants from him."

"I've hired Sherie Taylor to work here in the shop," Lily explained softly.

"Ah. I see," Coraline said, nodding. "I suppose she is a better match, but the potted plants are something for Kenneth, and everyone can't be hired."

"The Wilburs still have it mighty tough," Tate pointed out, "but I understand." He said the last to Lily, who smiled gratefully.

"I'll pray for the Wilburs," she offered, and Tate went out, waving a farewell.

Lily watched until his tall form disappeared from sight, quite forgetting that Coraline was there until she met that older lady's clear blue gaze.

"Oh, um, something to cheer an ailing friend, you said?"

"Daisies, I think. She has a fondness for daisies."

Lily got busy looking for an appropriate container, but while she was doing that, Coraline was looking at her. "Want to tell me about it?"

"About what?" Lily's fingers trembled over a selection of glass vases. She was no good at nonchalance.

"About whatever I interrupted when I came in just now."

Shrugging as casually as she could, Lily said, "You didn't interrupt. It was all over when you came in." She winced inwardly as that last came out.

"What was over, may I ask?"

Choosing a tall, sunny yellow vase with a fluted edge, Lily slowly turned to face the kind woman who had so quickly become a friend. "The kiss," she confessed, her cheeks heating. Coraline's eyes widened. "It was just a tiny kiss," Lily hastened to explain. "Barely a kiss at all, really."

Coraline straightened and a smile slowly spread across her face. "My dear," she said, "that's the best news I've had in a long while."

"It is?" Surprised but pleased, Lily smiled.

"Oh, my, yes. It's about time that boy started to fully live again. Now," she said, "if only you can get him to go to church."

"What do you mean?" Lily asked.

Coraline blinked at her. "Didn't you know? Tate Bronson hasn't set foot in church since the day he buried his wife."

Her heart in her throat, Lily pushed her rolling stool away from the stainless steel worktable and stood, calling out, "Be right with you!"

Across the table from her Sherie kept working on the simple corsages that they were making for a sweet sixteen party. It had been this way for the last couple of days. Every time the bell over the door rang, Lily rushed to see who had entered the shop, hoping against hope that it would be Tate. As before, Lily disguised her disappointment with a smile.

"Hello, Chief Sheridan. How may I help you?"

Joe Sheridan stowed his mirrored sunshades in

the front pocket of his blue uniform shirt and placed his hands on the counter. "I'm thinking I might cheer up my wife with some roses."

"I'm sorry to hear she needs cheering," Lily said, waving him over to the glass-fronted humidifier case. "What type of roses does she like?"

"Yellow ones are her favorites."

"I have some pretty yellow ones with reddish tips."

"Ooh, I bet she'd like those. How much?"

Lily quoted a price just above wholesale, and he knew it.

"I appreciate that, Ms. Farnsworth. What with the pay cuts and the layoffs, we're hanging on by our fingernails. That's the whole problem, you know. My Inez fears we'll be moving before long, and if the department is decommissioned, we will be. The few men I've got left have been applying for jobs all over the state, and I can't say as I blame them."

"I—I had no idea," Lily told him, choosing a dozen of the long-stemmed roses. She carried them to the counter and began wrapping them in waxy green paper.

"It's the same at the school, you know. Things don't turn around, the county will absorb our students, and this school will close."

Lily looked up at that. "Truly? It's that bad?"

"I'm afraid so." He ran a hand over his light brown crew cut. "But we've got hope now, don't we? I've seen more activity on Main Street this past week than I've seen in months."

Nodding, Lily smiled. "Hope and prayer, Chief Sheridan," she told him.

"A good combination," he agreed, handing over several dollar bills as payment.

Lily made change for him, thanked him for his business and bid him farewell. She didn't make it back to the worktable before the bell jingled again. Hurrying back the way she'd come, Lily put her smile on.

An older woman bent over a display of succulents. She wore a faded dress torn at the waist and athletic shoes with mismatched socks. Around one wrist twisted several lengths of dirty ribbon. Someone had attempted to braid her long, graying brown hair, but much of the wiry mess had escaped the plait to stick out at odd angles. She looked up and smiled, displaying empty spaces where teeth should be.

"Where do you keep the salad vegetables?" she asked brightly. "I do so like a good salad. Don't you?"

Lily glanced around. "This is a flower shop, ma'am. We don't carry vegetables."

As she spoke, the woman made a beeline for the humidifier. "Don't these look good? Yum."

"Oh, no," Lily exclaimed, alarmed. "These aren't for eating."

The woman laughed. "My son raises green ones this big!" She held up her hands six inches apart.

"Who is your son?" Lily asked, thinking that she should call the gentleman.

"John," she answered. "No, wait. John's my husband." She giggled at her mistake and flitted to a display of silk flowers. "Pretty," she murmured. "I could grow these."

Lily went over and took the woman's arm, steering her away from the glass shelves. "Ma'am, could you tell me your name, please?"

"My name?" The woman tapped her chin uncertainly. "Don't you know? One of us should know."

Lily gulped. Sherie appeared, leaned against the end of the workroom wall and calmly said, "Hello, Mrs. Wilbur."

"Oh, hello," the woman said. "Do I know you?"

"Yes, ma'am. I went to school with Kenneth."

"Kenneth?"

"Your son."

"Oh. No, I don't think so. My son's name is John."

Lily shared a look with Sherie and went to the phone. Unfortunately she received a message that the number Kenneth Wilbur had given her had been disconnected. Finances were obviously even worse for the Wilburs than she'd realized. She thought about calling the police department, but no crime had been committed, after all, and it wasn't exactly an emergency. Besides, she knew someone who could help, someone she'd been wanting to see again ever since he'd kissed her.

She went into the office and dialed Tate's cell phone. When he answered, she quickly apprised him of the situation.

"I'm sorry to bother you, but I have an unexpected visitor at my shop, a Mrs. John Wilbur, I believe."

"Are you telling me that she's alone?"

"Very much so, and when I called the phone number on Kenneth's employment application, it was disconnected."

Tate let out a long sigh. "Is she all right?"

"Confused. She came in looking for salad vegetables, and she seems to frighten easily. She didn't recognize Sherie, though they've apparently known each other a long time."

"I'll…find someone to inform Kenneth and come as quickly as I can. Maybe she'll know me."

Relieved, Lily went out to see how Mrs. Wilbur was doing. The poor thing was still browsing among the flowers and murmuring about lettuce.

"Ma'am," Lily asked, "are you hungry?"

Mrs. Wilbur turned and blinked owlishly. "Yes. Do you have vegetables?"

Lily made a decision. "No, ma'am, I'm afraid not, but we might have something else you'd like." She glanced at Sherie then. "I have to run out for a minute. Will you be okay here?"

Sherie smiled, her eyes cutting to the wall that separated the floral shop from the bakery.

"Sure. Mrs. Wilbur and I are old friends. We'll be in the workroom."

Lily squeezed her employee and new friend's shoulder then went out to prepare an impromptu tea party.

Chapter Eight

Sherie Taylor stood behind the counter when Tate pushed through the door into the florist's shop. She closed the lid on a box of corsages and handed them to Adele Chaplet, saying, "I hope the girls enjoy the party."

"The corsages are just beautiful," Adele gushed. "They're going to be thrilled." Adele went out, smiling at Tate.

"Sweet sixteen party," Sherie informed him. "Adele decided to give corsages as party favors."

Tate lifted his eyebrows. "That's a new twist. Where is she?"

Sherie pointed into the workroom, and he walked around the counter to peer around the wall. Lily sat at the stainless steel worktable next to Mrs. Wilbur. Both women held teacups in their hands, plates of half-eaten iced cakes and cookies in front of them, napkins in their laps. A vase of flowers sat in the center of a lace doily between them.

"Strawberry is my favorite," Mrs. Wilbur was saying. "Kenneth has a strawberry wagon. Did I tell you? It's his own design, glass sides, shelves inside, vents for directing the breeze. He turns it to catch the sun. We have strawberries nearly all year long."

"That's brilliant," Lily exclaimed. "I wonder if he'd make me one to sit out in front of the shop on the sidewalk. What a pretty display it would make. I bet we could sell them to order, too."

"He's clever, my Kenneth," Mrs. Wilbur said, smiling. She sounded perfectly normal, her old self. Tate watched as Lily reached over and squeezed her hand. "That boy can grow anything."

"So I'm told. I'm going to check out his herbs very soon, I promise you. Maybe he can teach me to grow some things. I know all about flowers, but I've only worked with them after they were cut. It might be fun to get in on the process at the beginning."

"Hmm, yes, flowers are lovely," Mrs. Wilbur agreed, "but you can't eat them." She sipped from her teacup and set it on the table.

"Can I get you another?" Lily asked.

Dabbing her lips with a napkin, Mrs. Wilbur shook her head. "No, thank you. That was delicious."

"I'll tell Mr. Smith you said so."

Tate stepped forward then, saying, "I didn't realize Smith provided tea."

Lily jerked around, her face lighting with a smile of such welcome that his heart turned over.

"He does," she said. "In fact, he has a lovely selection of teas."

Tate nodded as he ambled forward. "Mrs. Wilbur, it's nice to see you."

The older woman frowned, fear creeping into her gaze. "Do I know you?"

"Yes, ma'am. Tate Bronson."

"No," she said, pushing away from the table, suddenly agitated. "I don't know you."

Tate looked at Lily, who shrugged slightly and shifted a cake from her plate to Mrs. Wilbur's, saying, "You haven't finished your cakes, Mrs. Wilbur. Aren't they delicious?"

Mrs. Wilbur blinked and snatched the cake from the plate as if worried Tate would steal it from her. He backed away.

Lily slid off her stool and followed him, whispering, "She's been perfectly lucid ever since we sat down."

"It's the Alzheimer's," he told her softly. "Kenneth says it's unpredictable."

"Figured it was something like that."

Kenneth came rushing into the shop then, calling out, "Mom! It's Kenneth!"

Mrs. Wilbur wilted like a flower left too long in the sun without water. Dropping the cake, she jumped off the stool and ran into the other room, crying anxiously, "Kenneth! Kenneth!"

He caught her in his arms and held her against him. "It's okay. I'm here."

Clinging to him like a lost child, she trembled, but then he looked to Lily and spoke. "Thanks for looking after her. Danny and I were out mowing yards to raise some cash and had her with us. We didn't even realize she'd left the van. I'm sorry if she was a bother."

"No bother," Lily said kindly. "We had a lovely tea party, didn't we, Mrs. Wilbur?"

The older woman straightened and turned a shining face to Lily, nodding. "I had a nice time."

"I'm glad."

Mrs. Wilbur looked at her son then, patted his chest and announced, "Lily and I are going to plant a community garden."

Lily's mouth dropped open, and she literally reeled backward a step, but then a smile broke across her face. "What a wonderful idea!"

Tate smiled, assuming that Lily meant only to humor Kenneth's poor mother, but something passed between her and Kenneth in the next moment. It was almost an audible click in the air around them.

"You know, that just might work," Kenneth said slowly.

"I think so, too," Lily told him, sounding excited, "but I don't have the expertise to pull off something like this."

"I do," Kenneth stated bluntly, stroking his whiskered chin. "We might just have time."

"You're saying it can still be done? That it's not too late in the summer?"

"Yes, but there's no time to lose and much to organize."

"How can I help?"

"We need a site," Kenneth said, "workers, seeds—no, at this late date, seedlings would be best—water, compost... It'll have to be enclosed to protect against pests."

"A community garden could help feed those who most need help," Lily pointed out excitedly, "but we'll need lots of assistance to pull it off."

"I'll do all I can," Kenneth volunteered.

Lily looked at Tate and said, "Surely we could gather some donations to pay for Kenneth's time and expertise."

Tate could have hugged her. Donations. The people of Bygones might not have much, but they would give what they did have, and he knew exactly where to start. The Bronsons would kick in, of course, and he could think of a few others who could afford to contribute generously. It seemed to him that Robert Randall ought to want to make a sizable contribution to such a worthy cause. Closing his factory had placed so many of the citizens of Bygones in dire straits, after all.

Lily and Kenneth were talking about rounding up volunteers to get the project started, but Tate wasn't worried about that. People would come as soon as they heard.

"First things first, though," Kenneth said. "Until we have a site, we don't have a garden."

"Leave that to me," Tate announced.

Lily turned bright eyes on him. "Really?"

When she looked at him like that, how could he do anything but succeed? "I'll have it taken care of by tonight."

She beamed. Beamed. Kenneth was pleased, too. Tate barely heard what he said, though. Tate was aware that Kenneth spoke excitedly as he ushered his mother from the shop, planning aloud, but all Tate heard or saw was Lily.

"Thank you," she told him softly.

"No," he countered. "Thank *you*."

She, after all, had looked after Mrs. Wilbur and she had come up with the idea—or at least planted the idea—of a community garden, then she had seen a way to glean something tangible out of it for Kenneth. Plus she had given Sherie Taylor a job, and she was making a go of her shop. Time would tell whether or not it would be a smashing success, but he figured that she had a good chance, a real good chance, and that was good for the town. What could he do in the face of all that but go out to keep his word?

Besides, it was the only way to be certain that he wouldn't kiss her again.

He still didn't know how that had happened. One minute they'd been friends casually comforting each other, and the next, they were man and woman, keenly aware of the mutual attraction that he had never intended to let happen again. But then he'd never intended to think about another woman as often as he thought about Lily. He told himself that it was because of his position on the committee, that it was a matter of his responsibilities and Lily's importance—or rather, the importance of her business—to the town, but he couldn't deny the way his heart leaped when she smiled at him.

This was dangerous ground upon which he walked, for he had no intention of marrying again… unless… No, it wouldn't be fair to ask Lily to give up the possibility of having a child of her own. He wouldn't even think of it. His business with Lily had to do with the town, nothing more. Just the town. So he would do this for the town, and if it pleased Lily, why should he be sorry about that?

"Closing time," Tate announced, walking through the door of Lily's shop for the second time that day, his daughter on his heels.

Lily glanced at the clock on the wall behind her, the hours marked by the number of blossoms. Four minutes until six o'clock.

"Close enough," she decided, winking at Isabella.

Tate flipped the sign in the door window, while Isabella beamed a secretive smile.

"What's going on?" Lily asked, taking her keys from beneath the counter.

"We have something to show you," Isabella announced. "Isn't that right, Dad?"

Tate just smiled and started turning off lights. Lily closed up the office then followed Tate and Isabella out onto the sidewalk. Tate took her keys and locked the door to the shop then walked over and opened the front passenger door of his truck for her. After handing her back her keys, he put Isabella into her booster, closed Lily's door and walked around to slide in behind the steering wheel.

Traffic on Main Street was heavy enough to prevent him from making one of his careless U-turns. Instead he pulled away from the curb and headed east down the block to Granary Road, but no sooner did he turn right than Isabella protested.

"Da-a-d. Not this way."

Tate rolled his eyes, glancing into the rearview mirror. "It's almost dinner time."

"Da-a-d, I promised Bonnie."

"Okay, okay."

He whipped a right onto School Drive then turned left onto Bronson Avenue, only to immediately turn into the parking lot of The Everything. Instead of immediately parking, however, Tate guided the truck past the gas pumps and over an uneven patch, bringing it to a stop beside the Snow Cone Cabin.

Nothing more than a portable shed, the tiny building held a rudimentary business that dispensed shaved ice drenched in flavored syrup. Tate explained that it was open only during the warm months and owned and operated by a pair of school-teachers, Nancy and Mac Jacobs, who had a couple kids, including Isabella's little friend.

"We try to stop in at least once a week," he said, killing the truck engine. "Like everyone else, they're worried about the school closing and try to earn a little extra cash."

"I see."

He grinned. "Not yet, but you will." With that, he got out. Lily did the same then opened the door for Isabella. Tate was there to escort them to the window in the side of the small building.

Mac Jacobs and Bonnie met them with smiles. "What can I get you?" Mac asked.

Isabella had a rainbow cone, Tate went for coconut, Lily chose mixed berry.

Bonnie looked to her father and asked, "Daddy, can I go with them to the park?"

"Are we going to the park?" Lily asked Tate in surprise.

"We are," he confirmed with a nod and smile before looking to Mac Jacobs. "Bonnie is welcome to join us. We won't be long."

"Go ahead," Mac said to his daughter. "But just until I close up here."

She ran out a back door and around the building to join Isabella. Giggling, the girls headed for a line of trees just a few yards distant.

"Bonnie seems to know more about what's going

on than I do," Lily said, falling in beside Tate as they strolled along behind the girls.

He shrugged. "Those two are on the phone all the time. I thought it would be a few years before I'd have to contend with that, but it's happening earlier and earlier nowadays from what I'm hearing."

"And you have skillfully avoided telling me what we're doing," Lily noted.

Tate chuckled. "Just sightseeing. For now."

They followed a well-beaten trail through the tall trees and into a green glade. A shallow, irregularly shaped pond lay to the left. A pair of fat ducks paddled around its reedy shore. Lily recognized the gazebo and the playground where the girls headed. Picnic tables with attached benches had been tucked in among the trees.

"This is Bronson Park."

"So it is." He pointed to the boxy, two-story, sand-colored dressed-stone house in the distance. "That's Saul's house. Most of the rooms are used by the public library. It's only open a couple days a week now. Budget cuts."

"Oh, that's too bad."

"It is." He bit off a chunk of shaved ice and waved a hand while he processed it. "You'll notice the fenced yard around the house."

"Wrought iron. Very nice."

"And a sizable enclosed space," he pointed out. "Kenneth says it's even big enough for a nice-size garden."

Lily's eyes went wide. "Really? I mean, you found a site already?"

Tate grinned. "I called the mayor. He called the city council and Coraline Connolly." He chuckled. "She and I both called Robert Randall and a few others. Kenneth's been on the phone all afternoon, too."

"You know his home phone was shut off?"

Tate waved a hand. "That's been taken care of." Lily grinned at him, knowing perfectly well who had paid the past-due bill. Tate cleared his throat, mumbling, "Part of my contribution to the project."

Laughing, Lily asked, "*Part* of your contribution?"

He shrugged, tossed the remainder of his snow cone into a nearby trash barrel and grabbed her hand, saying, "Come on. I need to find a way to get a tractor through that fence."

Lily sent her snow cone after his, and they ran like children across the grass to the homestead. Tate told her that a man who used to work for the city maintenance crew reported that one of the wrought-iron panels would slide up out of position to allow equipment into the fenced area. They started at the front gate and worked their way around to the back, where they found the iron loops that held the removable section in place. Acting together, they lifted the section free and set it aside. Tate judged the opening adequate for the small tractor he had in mind to use to plow the ground.

While they were doing this, Mac Jacobs pulled his small SUV into the parking lot and honked the horn for Bonnie. The girls ran to obey, Bonnie climbing into the backseat of the SUV, Isabella joining her father and Lily as they surveyed the garden plot.

"When will you start?" Lily asked.

"Tomorrow morning," Tate said. "Folks will be here by dawn to start disking up the sod. Then I can plow and till in the fertilizer."

"Fertilizer?"

"That's right. Kenneth's already got nearly a ton of compost and manure coming."

"But how?"

Tate spread his hands. "That's the beauty of a small town. News spreads like wildfire, and when there's a need, everyone pitches in to help."

"I still can't believe you got it all going so fast," she exclaimed.

"Me? You're the one who got this ball rolling. Oh, I know that Mrs. Wilbur gave you the idea, but you realized instantly that a community garden could benefit the town's most needy and throw some work Kenneth's way. There's talk of letting him sell leftover harvest to provide ongoing funding, so this could turn into a self-sustaining project."

"Tate, that's wonderful!" Lily cried, throwing her arms around him.

The next thing she knew, Isabella had joined in, her small arms wrapping around Lily's and her father's legs. Lily froze, fearing that Tate would quickly pull away. Instead he threw back his head and laughed. Wrapping an arm around Lily's shoulders, he patted his daughter indulgently. Suddenly they were all laughing. In that moment life in Bygones felt almost unbearably sweet.

When Tate and Isabella arrived at the garden site just after seven o'clock on Saturday morning, they found that a sizable group had already gathered. Some—his parents, all three Wilburs, Coraline Connolly and the Garmans—Hugh, Wendy and grandson Matt included—had been at work since dawn. Josh Smith was on-site, giving out coffee from the back of his white van, along with rolls, courtesy of the Sweet Dreams Bakery. Almost before he got the tractor backed off the trailer, Tate heard that Patrick Fogerty, down at the Fixer-Upper, might put in an aboveground watering system later, once the plowing and planting had been finished.

Tate was halfway through the plowing when he spotted Lily among those hanging on the fence. She'd worn jeans and a loose blue T-shirt with a yellow bandana tied around the fluffy ponytail atop her head. Tate smiled to himself, wondering if she'd purposefully worn Bygones' blue and yellow school colors or if it had been a happy coincidence. He somehow thought it might have been on purpose.

She waved. Then Isabella did the same, followed by his parents. The Wilburs also waved, first Kenneth and Mrs. Wilbur, though Tate doubted she knew what she was doing or why. Then Danny Wilbur, Kenneth's teenage son, waved and his good buddy, Matt Garman, followed suit. The gesture moved around the perimeter of the garden, for no reason other than that he was doing something for the good of the community. Tate thought of the town motto, *"Family First."* They were all family in a way, one big family pulling together to do what was best for the town.

At the end of a row he spun the wheel, turning the tractor, and Lily came into view again. She smiled and shielded her eyes from the rising sun. He mused idly that he had a visor in the truck that he'd get for her as soon as he was finished here. Meanwhile, her smile felt as warm as morning sunshine.

He finished the plowing and pulled the tractor out of the way so the wagon load of freshly mixed compost could be hauled in on the back of a four-wheeled utility vehicle owned by the city. Tate went to grab the visor, returning to find Lily on the business end of a spade tossing manure-rich fertilizer.

"Give me that," Tate ordered, trying not to chuckle, "and put this on." He pitched the visor at her and started shoveling.

"Why, thank you," she told him brightly, and when next he looked up, she was raking the compost evenly over the ground just as Kenneth directed.

When Kenneth seemed satisfied that the layer had been distributed as evenly as possible, Tate changed the disks on the tractor and got back in the driver's seat. He went over the ground in all directions. By the time he was done, Kenneth had stakes ready to be hammered into the soil and lengths of string cut to be tied between them. While teams of four laid out planting rows, Kenneth went through and organized the seedlings that had come in from all over town. Meanwhile rolls of fine mesh-wire cloth arrived, and a group started figuring out how best to get it up inside the wrought iron in order to protect the tender seedlings from pests such as rabbits and groundhogs.

"Organized chaos," Lily said, coming to stand next to Tate.

"That about sums it up," he agreed with a grin and a nod.

"Just look at them, though," Lily went on, throwing out a hand, "all working together for a common goal."

Tate flicked a finger at the brim of her visor, teasing, "We're going to make a Bygonian out of you yet."

She put a hand on her hip, quipping saucily, "Is that anything like a begonia?"

He chuckled. "You tell me. I wouldn't know a begonia from a Bygonian."

"Well, allow me to educate you one of these days."

Absurdly, his heartbeat sped up to triple time. Their byplay couldn't have been more innocent, more public or more personal and significant. Somehow he was getting in deeper and deeper with her, and he didn't know how to stop it. Worse, far worse, he didn't want to stop it, but it couldn't go anywhere. Even if he decided to try marriage again, it would have to be with a woman who could be content with just him and Isabella.

When Kenneth called them over to the tailgate of the old truck where he had set up his office and was organizing the activity, Tate felt both glad and resentful for the interruption. Before ambling over with Lily, he checked first to be sure that Isabella still played happily with several other children whose parents had come along to lend a hand. He found himself thinking that he wouldn't mind having another child if it didn't have to be like last time. Bemused by that thought, he shook his head and took a place next to Lily, standing with arms folded and his hands safely tucked against his sides, his attention focused on Kenneth.

"I'm setting up a routine weekly schedule," Kenneth explained, "and I figured you two ought to get first dibs since you've been in on this thing from the get-go. So, which day and time work best for the two of you?"

The two of them? Tate looked at Lily and found her looking at him. She shrugged and said something about Sherie's normal days off. Alarmed, Tate barely heard her. Why was Kenneth treating them like a couple? They weren't a couple. They were…

He wasn't sure what they were. Just two people signing up to pull weeds. It wasn't as if they were getting married, after all. He rubbed his chin, trying to think.

"Um, Isabella goes over to spend the day with her grandparents early on Fridays right now. How does that sound?"

"That's good," Lily said.

"Earlier the better for me," he mumbled.

They settled on an hour that should have them there right about daybreak.

Isabella came running then. "Daddy, are you done now?"

"I think so. For today. Let's start loading up."

Isabella hugged Lily in farewell, saying, "Guess I'll see you tomorrow, huh?"

Lily chucked her under the chin. "Yes, sweetie. I'll see you in church tomorrow." Lily lifted her big blue eyes to Tate's face then, and he saw her gulp before she asked brightly, too brightly, "What about you, Tate? Won't you join us in church tomorrow?"

Isabella caught her breath, instantly brightening. Tate saw that the hope in his daughter's eyes equaled that in Lily's, and he knew that he could thrill them both by simply saying yes. He also knew that, ultimately, he must disappoint them both, however.

Oh, he could go to church. It wasn't a big thing. Once, it had seemed so. Now, somehow, it did not, except that if he went tomorrow, it would be for

Lily, and that *would* be a big thing. It was better not to build hopes that should not exist. Smoothly he said to Lily what he had so often said to others over these past years.

"I've claimed Sunday mornings as me time. It's the one day of the week when I can just go back to bed and stay there. Believe me, if you were a single parent, you'd understand how important that is. Most Sundays, I don't even shave."

He said the last with a chuckle, ignoring the fact that Isabella rolled her eyes. She knew perfectly well that he fed the livestock on Sundays and did all the chores that had to be done on a daily basis, but then he kicked back and often just burrowed down in front of the TV to watch whatever sports might be available.

Lily visibly shrank, her disappointment palpable. Tate felt a kick in his gut, a yawning emptiness that made him want to apologize and capitulate. He forced himself to turn away, but he couldn't help feeling like a scoundrel. He decided he'd make it up to her somehow. He'd find some less dangerous and compromising way to take that sad look off her face and put the smile back in its place, something that would not announce to the whole town, his daughter included, that Lily Farnsworth had somehow become important to him.

Chapter Nine

Sunday had lost some of its sparkle for Lily, but she tried not to let it show when she greeted Isabella the next morning, especially as others seemed particularly ebullient. Everyone buzzed about the great success of the Grand Opening on Monday and the community-wide hopes for the homestead garden. She still heard some contrary remarks. It hadn't even been a week since the opening, some cautioned. Others pointed out that the garden was only needed because folks were having trouble keeping food on the table. Still, a mood of thanksgiving and praise permeated the service, and Lily felt her spirit lifted despite her disappointment at Tate's refusal to attend church that morning.

Me time, he'd said.

She'd never heard anything so patently ridiculous coming from someone as selfless as Tate Bronson. Not only was he a dedicated single father, his devotion to his parents, friends and community testified that he seldom thought of himself. Why, he put the animals in his care before himself. She didn't believe for a minute that he stayed home from church out of some selfish desire to put himself before God and everyone else. No, he'd stayed away from church because he was angry with God for allowing his wife to die. At least that must have been the problem at first, but Tate didn't seem angry now.

She couldn't help feeling that Tate stayed away now because of her. Coraline had seemed to believe that Lily could get Tate back into church, but after thinking it over, Lily had come to the opposite conclusion. She had come to the conclusion that Tate's absence had become more a matter of habit than anything else. That being the case, almost anyone could get Tate back into church now *except* her.

She knew very well that he didn't want her to think that he might like her too well, that she might mean more to him than a friend and an asset to the town. That kiss had simply complicated things, made it less likely that he would respond as hoped to her invitation, not *more* likely as Coraline had assumed. No, she was the last person who might be able to get Tate Bronson back into church.

After the service Lily made a point of speaking to Isabella. With only a week until the girl's eighth birthday, Lily needed a bit of guidance. She wanted to give the girl a gift but an appropriate one, most especially one that wouldn't upset her father.

"So tell me, Isabella," she said, catching up to the

girl and her grandparents on the sidewalk in front of the church, "what are your birthday plans?"

"I'm having a tea party," Isabella replied excitedly. "You'll be there, won't you?"

Lily sidestepped that with a smile and a show of enthusiasm. "How wonderful! What would you like for your birthday?"

"A hamster," she exclaimed at once, lifting her shoulders. "They're so cute and cuddly. I seen 'em down at Fluff & Stuff. There's one that is sooo sweet. They got their own special houses, and they live in your room. They even got clothes and toys and things. Bonnie, she pushes hers around in a buggy, like her mom pushes her baby sister."

"That sounds like fun."

"Uh-huh. So that's what I want, a hamster of my own. I know just the one, too."

"Anything else?" Lily asked, thinking that Tate must be buying the hamster.

"Well…" Isabella drilled a toe against the sidewalk then blurted, "You said it yesterday. I really want Daddy to come to church on my birthday."

Ginny and Peter Bronson traded doubtful looks. Lily felt awful. If she hadn't brought it up, maybe Tate would have come to church on his daughter's birthday. If only she hadn't invited him in front of Isabella. She wished she hadn't invited him at all.

Gulping, she steered the conversation back to gifts. "Do you like roses?"

Isabella drew in her chin, her head tilting. "I like 'em, 'specially pink ones. Why?"

Lily put on a secretive smile sure to pique a little girl's interest. "Oh, no reason."

Ginny took her granddaughter's hand and led her away then. What Lily hadn't said was that she would like to give Isabella a rosebush to plant. That way she would always have roses. Lily just wasn't sure if that was an appropriate gift for an eight-year-old. Fortunately she got a chance to ask Tate when he showed up in her shop on Monday morning to hand deliver an invitation to Isabella's tea party, along with a beverage from the Cozy Cup Café.

"It's this Saturday," he said apologetically, placing the glittery pink envelope on the counter next to a tall container of coffee, "which may be short notice, but we couldn't make up our minds what to do this year. I mean, with so many folks struggling, it was hard to decide."

"I understand. You don't want anyone to feel obligated to buy a gift."

"Exactly. On the other hand, it's Isabella's birthday, and her friends' parents kept saying how much everyone was looking forward to a party." Tate pushed back his hat. "Mom's going to provide a dress-up box. Then the girls will have some sort of fruit tea and cakes from the Sweet Dreams Bakery, and I was told to be prepared to paint fingernails. I even heard something about fingernail jewelry."

Laughing, Lily opened the envelope and read the invitation. "I'll be there to help out any way I can."

Tate clapped a hand to his chest. "Thank you."

Still grinning, Lily peeked beneath the slanted cap of the coffee cup and caught her breath. "Caramel macchiato! It is, isn't it?"

Looking up, Tate gave her a crooked smile. "I thought a city girl from Boston might appreciate something fancy. Josh called it a a caramel cold brew, I think."

Lily took a long drink of the sweet, cold, flavored coffee, sighing with pleasure. "Bygones doesn't know how blessed it is."

Tate chuckled. "Am I forgiven for roping you into helping give an eight-year-old a birthday tea party then?"

Lily pretended to consider then nodded. "Totally."

"Whew!" He wiped imaginary perspiration from his brow. "Does that mean you'll also clue me in on this hamster stuff?"

Lily shrugged. "All I know is what your mom must have heard."

"Mom thought it sounded like Isabella wants a *certain* hamster."

"Yes, that's what it sounded like to me, too."

Tate spread his hands. "Well, how am I supposed to know which hamster?"

Lily couldn't answer that. "Maybe the best thing

to do is to take her hamster shopping. Let her pick out her own hamster."

"Now, that's an idea," Tate said. "You know, when we were down at the pet store before, I noticed that some of the hamster paraphernalia, the toys and things, were pretty cheap, and if Isabella already had a hamster, I could tell her friends' moms to pick up that stuff as gifts."

"You could," Lily agreed.

"Okay, then," Tate decided, nodding, "we'll go hamster shopping."

"That's great," Lily said. "I'll buy her something *hamsterish,* too, then."

"Oh, no," he objected at once. "She's expecting roses from you."

"I—I had thought about giving her a rosebush to plant, but…"

"That's a wonderful idea," Tate said. "Really. She'd like that. She has a thing about butterflies, you know, and roses draw butterflies, don't they?"

"Well, most flowers do, I guess. I thought I'd have Kenneth advise me and then Isabella could pick a spot to plant her bush."

"That's cool. She'll get a kick out of that."

Lily smiled into her iced coffee. "It's settled then."

Tate sighed contentedly and resettled his hat on his head before taking his leave. So far, Lily thought, things were going just fine in Bygones, better than she'd thought they might at first.

* * *

Isabella tilted her head to view the writing stenciled on the wide gold ribbons spread atop the stainless steel table in Lily's workroom.

"Gone to Glory. What's that mean?"

"Heaven," Tate said with an indulgent smile. "It means, gone to Heaven."

"So somebody died?" Isabella asked tentatively.

"She was an elderly Christian lady," Lily explained gently. "Her son is your grandpa's age, and he said she was happy that her time finally came to go to Heaven."

Isabella looked at Tate and said, "Mama must like it in Heaven a whole lot."

He felt broadsided, never having considered that before. He'd thought only of what Eve had missed, not getting to see their daughter grow and learn, not having the chance to learn from her. And to think he'd tried to keep Isabella out of here this morning. She'd been agitating for Lily to join them on their hamster-shopping adventure since he'd first mentioned it, and he'd been subtly trying to dissuade her ever since.

He was suddenly glad that he hadn't managed to do so. He'd have missed this particular lesson. Feeling rather humbled, he waved a hand at the flower arrangement blanketing the worktable.

"Eversleigh appears to be keeping you busy."

Lily nodded. "Two orders this week, and it's only Tuesday."

"I hadn't heard," Tate said with a frown.

"Both are from the county, outside of town."

"Ah."

"You're coming, though, aren't you?" Isabella asked anxiously. "You're not too busy? Daddy says you're too busy, but you're not, are you?"

Lily sent a helpless look to Tate. He whacked his cap against his thigh and enlightened her. "Hamster shopping."

"Ah." Lily caught Sherie's eye. "Can you handle things here?"

"Absolutely," Sherie told her. "You go on. Just don't forget that Gracie Wilson and Mrs. Morgan will be in to discuss wedding flowers at two."

"Can we have pizza for lunch first, Daddy?" Isabella asked.

Caught, Tate forced a smile and capitulated. "Sure."

"Best invitation I've had all day," Lily said, rising and reaching behind her to untie the strings of the dark green apron that she wore over her gauzy skirt, white, and a simple short-sleeved pink T-shirt. "Can I bring you anything, Sherie?"

"No, thanks. I carried my lunch from home today. Happy hamster shopping."

"You are a treasure," Lily said, hurrying around

the table to join Tate and Isabella, who practically hopped up and down in her eagerness.

They went out with Sherie merrily calling behind them, "Takes one to know one!"

"I have to admit," Tate said, pulling the door closed behind them, "Kenneth wouldn't have worked out half so well as Sherie."

Lily shot him a grateful glance. "Things have a way of working out, don't you think? When you put your trust in the right place."

He knew she wasn't talking about him putting his trust in her, though he could certainly do that. No, she was letting him know that she'd prayed sincerely about the situation, and it had worked out for the best, just as Coraline and the others had prayed about the town's situation and along had come an anonymous benefactor willing to help them attract new businesses to town. He was going to have to think seriously about that trust soon, but not just now, not yet.

They stepped out onto the sidewalk, and Isabella took Lily's hand. She reached back for his, too, but Tate hesitated, stubbornly thinking of Eve, of the look of joy on her face as a squalling, infant Isabella had been laid in her arms and then of the way she had jerked and her eyes had rolled before she'd grabbed her head and started to gag. A nurse had thrust Isabella into his arms and shoved the pair of them out of the way. It had been just the two of them ever since. Eve had "gone to Glory."

He had missed her so much. He wondered when he had stopped missing her and why he couldn't make himself miss her anymore.

Mama must like it in Heaven a whole lot.

He knew it was true. Taking his daughter's plump, warm hand in his, he knew it was true.

Because of the busyness of Main Street, he'd had to park around the corner on Bronson Avenue. It would have been foolish to climb into the truck just to turn around and drive half a block to The Everything, so they walked, crossing the alley behind the Main Street stores, then School Drive. They entered the building through the convenience store. Elwood greeted them, as usual, from behind the counter.

"We're going hamster shopping after lunch, Mr. Dill," Isabella announced.

Elwood shook his head, stroking his chin whiskers. "Now, don't that beat all? I wouldn't have figured that pet shop would work for nothing. Shows what I know."

They wound their way through the shelves of small products and past the drinks cooler into the uneven hallway that connected the convenience store part to the grill part of the business, coming out between the order counter and another drinks cooler. Four mismatched tables, each with four chrome-and-hard-blue-vinyl chairs, occupied what space was not taken up by the tiny kitchen area. Velma Dill sat atop a stool behind the order counter reading, of all things, a fashion magazine. She quickly tossed it aside.

"What can I get for you?"

They ordered a full pepperoni pizza and went to choose bottled drinks from the cooler, which they carried to a table and opened to enjoy while the microwave ticked down the minutes. Velma cut the pizza, returned it to its box, added paper plates and napkins and bagged the whole lot. Tate paid, and they left to eat beneath the trees in the park behind the building.

The pizza tasted surprisingly good until it cooled and became too tough to chew. Even then, the ducks were happy to have the crusts, much to Isabella's delight. The breeze blew steadily enough to make sitting in the shade at midday quite pleasant even in mid-July. Sitting across from him, Lily tucked their refuse into the plastic bag and tied it up tightly before turning on the attached bench of the picnic table to lean back, hanging her elbows on the tabletop and stretching out her slender legs. She crossed her ankles, the delicate ruffled hem of her skirt at satisfying odds with the practical canvas of her slip-on shoes.

Her long blond hair pooled upon the tabletop in glossy waves. Tate felt a surprising urge to comb his hands through it. He might have done so if his daughter hadn't been there. Tate held out the bag of trash to her. "Take care of this so we can go."

Isabella ran off to do as instructed. Lily half turned on the bench seat.

"I've eaten better pizza," she said through a smile, "but never enjoyed one more."

He knew exactly how she felt. Watching Isabella on the way back to the table, he couldn't remember when he'd felt such simple joy, not since... He couldn't actually think of a time when he'd felt this comfortable, easy happiness.

Moments of ecstatic delight came to him: the moment Eve had agreed to be his steady girl, their wedding day, the night Eve had told him she was pregnant, Isabella's birth. In between had been lots of ups and downs, some fun, some worry, plenty of hard work. It seemed to him now that it had all gone so fast that they'd hardly had time to enjoy the important moments. Maybe that had been his fault. Everyone had been concerned that he and Eve had married too young, so he'd felt that he had to prove them wrong. Well, he had nothing to prove now.

As Isabella drew near, he and Lily rose. They began to stroll across the block-long park. When they reached the sidewalk on Granary Road, they turned left and walked on past School Drive, the alley and the end of the tan-painted brick building that housed the shops. Another left and a simple matter of a few steps took them to the door of the pet store, with its dark red trim.

It was an interesting shop with a lot to see, and as eager as Isabella had been to buy her hamster, she took her time getting to that section of the store where she could take her pick. She talked to the parrot and tried to pet the cagey old cat that slinked about the place. Once she got to the hamsters, however, she required only a moment to choose a dark orange bit of fur almost as red as her own head.

"That's a pumpkin Russian," Chase Rollins, owner of Fluff & Stuff, informed them. "He's a bit larger than most dwarfs and a spunky one. He can make that hamster wheel fly."

"Spunky," Isabella crooned, cuddling the little fellow close. "That's a good name." The critter promptly crawled inside her shirt, sending her into gales of laughter. Lily fished the hamster out again.

They set about choosing a habitat, which consisted of a pair of chambers and the requisite connecting pipe, all translucent. Next came bedding, food and various other items deemed immediately necessary. Nearly an hour passed before they went out again, arms filled, to walk up Main Street to Lily's shop. Isabella carried Spunky in a cardboard carton folded to resemble a house, while Tate and Lily carried the supplies.

"Maybe I should've brought the truck, after all," Tate muttered, toting bags.

"You know, I've been thinking," Lily said conversationally. "I'm going to have to buy a delivery van. Eversleigh has been sending over a car for flowers, but with the Wilson wedding coming up, I have to think ahead."

"New or used?" he asked.

"Definitely used, and nothing too big or flashy. All I really care about is dependability."

"In that case, Kenneth's had a minivan for sale for some time now."

"Really? That's…fortuitous."

"I'll ask him if he's still interested in selling and, if so, set up a meeting."

"Yes, do that."

"What about a delivery person?"

"I hadn't really thought about that. I do drive, but there might be times when I can't get away from the shop or need an extra pair of hands."

"Danny is a nice, dependable young man."

Lily slanted a smile in his direction. They entered the flower shop a moment later.

At least fifteen minutes remained before the hour of two o'clock, but Mrs. Morgan's supercilious voice could be heard complaining all the same.

"…biggest wedding of the year," she was saying. "You'd think the proprietor would have the courtesy to be available."

Tate frowned at the woman, disliking the look of dismay on Lily's face. Gracie came forward at the sound of the bell to greet Lily. "We're early. I hope it's not inconvenient."

"Not at all," Lily said, ever gracious.

"Ah, you have returned," Mrs. Morgan announced flatly. "We need more flowers." She essentially waved Gracie out of the way as if she was of no consequence and addressed Lily directly. "What Grace has chosen so far is not adequate."

Paper thin, artificially tanned and sleekly styled, this attractive wife of a successful surgeon never failed to let everyone know that she routinely traveled to Manhattan, Kansas, where her husband practiced, to shop and have her hair done. Now she meant to see that her son, Trent, had the wedding of the year even if it meant paying for it herself. Tate watched Gracie duck her head in embarrassment and knew he had to do something. Reaching for the bags that Lily still held, he murmured that he needed to speak with her for a moment.

"Excuse me, please," she said, stepping away from Mrs. Morgan and Gracie.

Tate bent his head to whisper in her ear. "Gracie's family can't afford a big splashy wedding, and Gracie isn't a big splashy kind of girl, but that's what the Morgans want, so Mrs. Morgan is paying. That leaves the bride with no say in her own wedding."

"I see," Lily said quietly. "I'll do what I can. Now, why don't you put those things in the truck while Isabella and Spunky wait here?"

Tate glanced around at a roomful of curious feminine eyes and did as he was bade. As he left, he heard Lily say, "You know, just before I came to Bygones, my sister married into one of the most prominent families in Boston. I happen to have some of her wedding photos, if you're interested."

Remembering that Lily had delayed her arrival

until after her sister's wedding, he hurried to deposit Isabella's birthday haul in the backseat of his truck cab. When he returned to the shop, he found Mrs. Morgan poring over Lily's photos.

"It's the style that all the upper echelon are using now," Lily was saying, "and it's the simplicity that makes it so very elegant."

"Well, of course it is," Mrs. Morgan said with a delicate sniff.

"Orchids are very expensive, though, aren't they?" Gracie asked.

Lily answered with a noncommittal "Um," then added, "Laurel chose orchids because she's allergic to other flowers. The daisies you chose would work just as well."

"I think we'll have roses," Mrs. Morgan decided, "yellow and red, as those are the truest colors."

"Pale yellow would be stunning with the crystal ribbon that you like," Lily pointed out gently, addressing Gracie, "and it so happens that I have it on hand." She turned to Mrs. Morgan then, saying, "It's a sparkling white so fine that it's translucent. I bought all of it I could find for my sister's wedding, so we couldn't be copied, you know. This far from Boston, however, I'm sure my sister won't object if I allow you to benefit from her exclusivity."

Mrs. Morgan preened, obviously mollified. Tate watched as Gracie and Lily surreptitiously traded conspiratorial looks. It didn't take a genius to figure out that Gracie had already picked out the crystal ribbon and Lily had just guaranteed that she would get at least that. Meanwhile, Lily would do all she could to rein in Mrs. Morgan's pretentious taste. Tate's admiration for the town's florist grew.

He signaled to Isabella, who was playing with her hamster on the counter, teasing him with a fern frond that had fallen from one of the plants. Lily excused herself from rescuing as much of Gracie's wedding as she could long enough to speak to them before their departure.

"Thank you for lunch and including me in the hamster expedition."

Isabella hugged her, Spunky's carton clutched tightly in one hand. "See you on Saturday."

"Absolutely."

"I'll let you know what I find out about the van," Tate told her.

"I look forward to hearing from you."

He winked, surreptitiously jerked a thumb at the table where Gracie and Mrs. Morgan waited and mouthed the words *good work.*

Lily just smiled and rocked up onto her toes. He couldn't help himself. He bent forward and kissed her cheek. The pleased, hopeful look on his daughter's face was enough to make him regret the gesture at once, but that didn't knock the smile off his face or keep him from looking forward to seeing Lily again.

He was getting in deeper and deeper, and he just couldn't seem to help himself.

Chapter Ten

Lily hugged that second kiss to her in a way that she had not dared do with the first. It had just been a peck on the cheek, but the warmth and affection of it simply could not be disputed. She could have done without the speculation in Gracie's and Sherie's eyes afterward, but the shock and deference that the kiss brought to Mrs. Morgan were both welcome. The Bronsons were still the "first family" of Bygones, but while status seemed to mean little to them, it obviously meant much to Mrs. Morgan. In addition to the wedding flowers, she placed a standing order for a monthly floral arrangement to grace her dining table.

The news quickly spread around town. Lily didn't think anyone had gossiped, exactly—well, not Sherie or Gracie, anyway. Still, Coraline Connally was well informed when she picked up Lily for the midweek service on Wednesday evening.

"I knew that boy was taken with you a week ago."

"It was a kiss on the cheek," Lily pointed out dismissively, but she couldn't hide her smile, so she stared out the rear passenger seat window of the sedan.

"In public," Miss Mars added with great portent from the front.

Lily rolled her eyes, but that smile stubbornly stayed put.

"You will continue to invite him to church, won't you?" Coraline asked, eyeing Lily via the rearview mirror.

"I'm not sure that's a good idea," Lily told her. "Why don't you invite him?"

"I *have* invited him," Coraline said. "I've reasoned with him, cajoled him. I've pleaded with that boy, if you must know, and he had no trouble telling me to mind my own business."

Lily leaned forward, frowning. "How long ago was that?"

"Oh…two, three years, at least, if not longer."

Sitting back, Lily shook her head. "I see. Well, if he won't go to church for his daughter's birthday, then I think it's safe to say that he won't go to church, period."

"Hmm," Coraline said, only that, until they pulled into the parking space in front of the church. "We will continue to pray about it and see what God is doing. Yes?"

"But of course," Miss Mars agreed.

"Yes." Lily added her soft voice to those of her friends.

She would definitely pray that Isabella's birthday wish would be granted. As for her and Tate, she didn't know what to think. Was he reconsidering his decision not to remarry? Was he open to the possibility? And what of children? If Tate could find his way back to church, then perhaps he could find enough faith to risk having a second child. Or was she once again spinning castles in the air around a man who could never be hers because, as dear as Isabella was, Lily didn't think she could be content without having a child with Tate?

The absurdity of that made her want to laugh—or weep. For years she'd despaired of ever even being noticed by a man, and now that someone seemed to have noticed her, she knew in her heart of hearts that it wouldn't be enough just to have a man want her or even marry her. For Lily marriage had to include a family and babies. Plural. A single kiss and a peck on the cheek didn't seem like much by comparison, at least not to her, but it was enough to cause talk.

Either Tate hadn't heard the talk by Thursday morning or he wasn't bothered by it, for he called to say that they could go over to look at Kenneth's minivan at any time convenient to her. Lily arranged for Tate to pick her up after the shop closed that evening, expecting that he would have Isabella with him. Tate arrived alone, however, having left Isabella with her grandparents.

Lily had taken a few minutes before Sherie left for the day to run upstairs and freshen up, exchanging jeans and a cotton blouse for white knit capris and a bold silky gold-and-white print, knee-length top. Gold flip-flops and a narrow gold headband completed the outfit. She almost changed her mind about it when Sherie whistled after she came back downstairs.

"Get a load of you! Wow. That's pretty classy for small-town Kansas."

"Too much?" Lily asked, looking down at herself and wrinkling her nose.

Sherie waved away her concern. "You look great. Tate won't know what hit him."

Lily's face flamed. "Uh, Tate's not... That is, I'm seeing about buying a van. I—I just want to make a good impression."

Grabbing up her purse, Sherie just grinned and headed for the door. "Uh-huh. I'd say you've got that covered. Hope the van thing goes well, too."

Lily gulped, nodded and managed a farewell wave as her employee went out, chortling. She passed Tate on his way in.

"Am I late? Got held up by a septic hog. Beats everything I've ever seen. One day it's fine, the next it's—" He broke off, shoved back the brim of the faded cap that he wore and looked her over before glancing down at his own muddy boots and dusty jeans. "Can you hold on for a minute? Uh, just close up while I…uh…" With that he spun and went right back out the door.

Lily groaned. Why hadn't she gone with the jeans and T-shirt? Why did she have to try to impress him? She considered going upstairs to change, but how would she explain that? She started turning off lights and shutting down the register. When she looked up a few seconds later, she spied him cutting across the street, sans cap, to the This 'N' That with a pair of jeans and a clean shirt on hangers. Was he going to change? For her? She couldn't help feeling flattered, especially as he jogged across the street four or five minutes later in fresh garments, his boots darkened as if he'd washed them in Miss Mars's restroom sink.

"Good thing I keep clean clothes in the truck," he said, coming through the door. "Can't hold a candle to you, but at least I won't embarrass you."

"You could never embarrass me!" she told him, blushing with the compliment.

"Why, thank you, ma'am," he drawled, bowing slightly. "But a fella likes to think he at least has a chance to keep up with a beautiful woman."

Lily caught her breath, embarrassingly close to tears. A beautiful woman. Her? No one had ever before called her beautiful, and she wasn't silly enough to believe it. She wasn't beautiful. Just a hopelessly smitten idiot.

* * *

They drove over to the Wilbur house on the north-west edge of town. The small clapboard structure stood almost hidden in the center of a large, double lot filled with a sizable garden, various sheds and detached garages. Tate explained that Kenneth did his own mechanic work and built planters for sale from salvaged materials, as well as bicycles, which he cobbled together from used parts. Lily took an instant liking to a rusty silver bike with a blue front fender.

Kenneth handed over the keys to the minivan and suggested that Danny go along to answer any questions they might have on the test drive. The boy made a valiant effort to sell the thing. Lily had driven several miles out of town and was on the way back again before Tate discovered what Lily had already realized.

"This is your vehicle, isn't it, Danny?"

"Um, it's the one I drive most," the boy evaded. "Dad's got to have the truck for hauling stuff. Besides, it's been rebuilt so much it's hardly worth anything at all. This here is a quality van. All the parts are original, and we have all the maintenance records, so the extended warranty is still in effect. Oh, and the seats come in and out real easy. I can show you when we get back to the house."

"That's fine," Lily said with a nod.

Tate wished the boy didn't have to part with his vehicle. Danny was a good son, though. He'd do what was needed without complaint, the same way he worked the garden and looked after his grandmother.

Back at the Wilbur place, they all got out and walked around the van, metaphorically kicking the tires. Kenneth stood back while Danny tried to close the sale, showing Lily how to remove the backseats inside the van to increase the cargo space.

"All right," Lily said. "I'll take it."

Neither Kenneth nor Danny immediately reacted, which caused her to look to Tate in confusion. He leaned close and said, "You should make a counteroffer to their asking price. That's how these things are done."

"Oh." She cleared her throat and offered fifty bucks less than the asking price. Tate literally gasped, but it was too late to suggest she try for five hundred less.

Kenneth and Danny traded incredulous looks and both yelled, "Yes!"

Lily nodded as if completely satisfied, and in a stern voice started laying out conditions. "Now, then, I'll want that silver bicycle thrown in. Oh, and, Danny, I'll be needing you to make deliveries. The hours are uncertain. I'll simply need you when I need you. Meanwhile, of course, I don't have a garage, so the van will have to stay with you. I'll pay for the insurance, but I'll expect you to keep the van gassed and ready. The pay is low,

I'm afraid, but you'll be free to keep any tips that you receive."

Danny stood with his mouth hanging open for a full ten seconds before he shifted and asked, "I can keep it here?"

"And drive it. If you're careful."

The kid put his hands to his head and twisted away, but not before Tate caught the shimmer of tears in his eyes.

Lily cleared her throat. "I, uh, need you and the van together if you're going to make the deliveries for me," she pointed out. "You do have a cell phone, don't you?"

He dropped his hands and turned, head and shoulders slowly bowing. "No."

Lily made a face. "Well, I have a business plan and an extra phone. Nothing fancy. We can add you to it. But you'll have to be responsible about your phone use."

Danny's head jerked up. He looked like he'd just received an electric shock.

"Danny's very responsible," Kenneth said quickly, his voice full of gravel.

"Well, then," Lily concluded briskly, "I can leave a deposit and take the bicycle today. Then we can complete the transaction early next week."

Kenneth insisted that a deposit was not necessary, and he agreed to drive with Lily to his bank in Manhattan on Tuesday to have the title changed and funds paid.

"Wait'll I tell Matt!" Danny suddenly exclaimed. His face colored, and he shifted his feet, adding, "It's just, well, we sort of been praying about selling the van."

Lily smiled and nodded. Tate loaded the bicycle into the truck bed, handed Lily up into the front seat, said goodbye to his friends and calmly drove away from the Wilbur place. He saw son and father embrace as he did so, clapping each other on the back. Long minutes passed before he trusted himself to speak around the lump in his throat.

"That was a good thing you did back there."

Lily shook her head. "I couldn't take his van away from him, especially as it was just going to sit at the curb in front of my shop ninety percent of the time." She rubbed her nose and straightened. "Besides, I know what it's like to have to give up a vehicle you love." She cleared her throat and added, "I sold mine to raise the matching funds to get the grant to come here."

Tate had to let that rattle around inside his mind for a minute or two. When he'd extracted all the implications from it, he said, "I somehow don't think that was a seven-year-old minivan."

She gave him a wry smile. "More like a BMW Z8 Roadster. Late model. Red."

Tate whistled. "That's a top-end vehicle."

"It was a graduation gift from my grandparents."

"Graduation gift? From what? Is there a flower design school?"

She took a deep breath and let it out again. "Law school."

He nearly ran the truck off the road. "You're a *lawyer?*"

She literally cringed. "I was. But I'm not now, not really. Don't tell anyone. I hated it, and that's why I quit, but my family... You have to understand. I'm the lowly *florist* in a family of lawyers. Oh, I'm saying it badly."

"Your whole family are lawyers?"

She nodded. "My grandfather is a judge." While he digested that, she went on. "My grandmother and father are law professors. My mother works for the Justice Department. My sister is in general practice in Massachusetts. As a matter of fact we used to practice at the same law firm. Then I saw this newspaper story about a town in Kansas offering grants to get businesses to locate there. I mean, here."

Tate shook his head. "No wonder your application was so well-prepared."

Lily sighed. "The truth is, I was a horrible failure as an attorney, and I just couldn't pretend anymore once my sister became engaged to—" She broke off, gasping back whatever she'd been about to say, but Tate wasn't about to let her stop there.

"Engaged to," he prodded, switching his gaze back and forth between the street and her, "engaged to who?"

"Er, her husband. I mean, the man who would become her husband."

"Lily," Tate said, "you're leaving out something. What are you leaving out?"

She covered her face with her hands. "He was our boss."

Tate tilted his head, trying to hear what she still wasn't saying. "So your sister married the boss. What's the big deal? Happens all the time."

Dropping her hands, Lily nodded miserably and confessed, "I had a terrible crush on him."

Tate hit the brake, causing the truck to stop several feet short of the four-way stop sign. He corrected the distance, thinking aloud. "So, your sister stole your boyfriend?"

"No! He hardly knew I existed. I told you, I'm not the sort of woman that men notice. Laurel is. He had his eye on her from the minute she first walked through the door. It was inevitable, really, and I'm happy for them. I—I just didn't want to hang around and watch them being happy together." Head bowed, she smoothed the hem of her top.

Grimly Tate made the left turn and guided the truck to the curb in front of Lily's shop. As soon as he put the transmission into Park, Lily erupted.

"I'm a terrible person, aren't I? My baby sister marries some guy I like a lot, so I run off to Kansas! It's pathetic."

"No. It's perfectly understandable." Tate felt the words burn in his throat. "If you love the guy and he marries your sister…"

"I don't *love* him," Lily scoffed, her head still

bowed. "I never loved him. I know that now." Her voice dropped to a whisper. "I just wanted him to notice me. Instead he noticed her."

"There must be something wrong with him," Tate told her, "because *I've* noticed you. I can't seem to help noticing you. And I don't understand how you can say you're a terrible person when you do things like you did this evening."

She smiled, shook her head and pushed up her glasses. "It's a good arrangement for everyone."

"Especially Danny," Tate pointed out. She shrugged, and he killed the engine. "I'll unload the bike for you."

"Would you mind taking it upstairs? I might paint it later."

"Not at all. Say, what are you doing for dinner?"

"Oh, I have a casserole ready to warm in the microwave," she said, glancing at him. "Would you, um, c-care to join me? There's plenty."

The sensible thing to do, of course, would be to make his excuses and go on his way, but he'd tossed aside sensible some time ago. Besides, Isabella had certainly already eaten with his parents. Why eat alone when he really wanted to spend this time with Lily, who had just done one of the nicest things he'd ever witnessed? What kind of fool wouldn't notice a woman like her?

"Don't mind if I do," he said, pulling the door handle.

Smiling, Lily did the same on her side. He lifted

her bicycle out of the bed of the truck and carted it up the stairs for her. While she got dinner going, he looked around the apartment, taking note of the unusual red furniture and dark yellow trimmings. She'd come up with curtains from somewhere, dark yellow with a red design printed on them.

"I like what you've done with the place," he called to her. She stuck her head out of the kitchen and smiled at him.

"Thank you. Miss Mars has been collecting bits and pieces for me."

"I've never seen anything like your living room furniture."

Lily chuckled. "You mean, you've never seen anyone paint outdoor furniture and use it inside before?"

He took a second look. "So that's it. Wow. I didn't even recognize it."

"Same with this," she said, carrying two plates, napkins and flatware to the round glass-topped dining table. She had no chairs for the table, just wood stools that she had painted and topped with cushions that matched her curtains. "Hope you like mac-and-cheese casserole and salad."

"Sure. Who doesn't?"

She went back to the kitchen. He stepped over to examine a framed photo on the wall. The girl in the strapless wedding gown looked a lot like Lily but with less natural beauty and more artificial polish. Her long hair had been professionally streaked and straightened and her makeup carefully done, but she lacked the lithe ballerina's build and the wholesome, unconscious loveliness that was Lily. This young woman looked worldly and...like every other attractive blonde. She simply wasn't as sweet and special as the maid of honor beside her. Lily looked slightly uncomfortable in a long strapless dove-gray dress, her hair swept up atop her head, fancy earrings dangling from her earlobes. He wished he'd been there to give her a hug and tell her to relax.

Hearing her emerge from the kitchen again, he said, "You're not wearing your glasses in this photo."

"I do have contact lenses, but I have problems with the solutions you have to store them in, so I don't wear them very often."

"I see. Just as well, if you ask me. I like the glasses. I like the way they look on you."

"Oh. Thanks." She blushed very prettily. Gesturing at the photo, she said, "They didn't go with the outfit, though, especially not with those earrings." She turned back to the kitchen.

He chuckled and moved to the table, where she had placed a steaming casserole and cool salad bowl. "You can choose the earrings for your own wedding," he said, raising his voice. "That's what Eve told her bridesmaids when we got married."

A long silence followed, during which even he froze. Had he really just said that so easily?

Lily came out of the kitchen carrying two tall glasses of iced water. He bent and pulled out one of the stools for her before taking the glasses from her grasp and placing one at each of the place settings.

"Looks good," he told her, dropping down onto his own stool.

"Thank you," she said, bowing her head and folding her hands.

A moment ticked by before he understood that she was praying. Suddenly he realized that she'd been giving thanks before her meals all along. He hadn't caught on before because she was so quiet about it and because she so often bowed her head. Now he realized that before every meal, she bowed her head and went quiet for a few seconds. He felt small and foolish and yet somehow *right* about it. She looked up, smiled and reached for the salad tongs.

For lack of anything else to talk about, he asked about her sister's wedding and received a blow-by-blow account that would have bored him to tears under other circumstances. His tears were tears of laughter, however, given Lily's witty telling of the "great engagement announcement," during which two people choked—Lily and the senior partner at the law firm—and the "invitation list wars," wherein the bride's mother and the groom's settled their guest list via professional arbitration.

Tate also learned that Lily had worked for a florist after earning a bachelor's degree in design and then while she attended law school at her family's behest. Later, because of her recommendation, the family had chosen her former employer to provide the flowers for her sister's wedding. Lily had volunteered to oversee the project, and the same florist who had once employed Lily had shown her the article about Bygones' Heart of Main Street grant project, which had given Lily the idea of applying for the grant.

"And here we are," Tate said, pushing back his now empty plate to rest his folded forearms against the edge of the table.

"And here we are," Lily said.

"I'm glad. I'm really glad." Glancing around, he saw that night had fallen. "Here," he said, rising to his feet. "Let me help you clean up so I can go. I've got an injured hog I need to check on before I can call it a day."

"No, no," she refused, staying his hands as he reached for the plates. "I'll take care of it. You go on. I'm just glad you stayed. Eating alone all the time gets old."

"I can see how it would, but I thank you all the same. I'll be seeing you at the garden in the morning."

She followed him to the entry. "That's right. On my new bike."

He opened the door and let himself out onto the landing. "Don't forget about the party on Saturday."

"Don't worry," she told him, following him out. He started down the stairs. "I won't leave you alone with all those little fingernails to paint," she teased.

He paused, turned, walked back up the stairs and wagged a finger in her face. He'd intended to say something clever, something witty and smart, but when he saw her standing there with that relaxed, happy smile on her face and those deep blue eyes shining behind the lenses of those cute round glasses, every word, every thought went right out of his head except one. He swept his arm around her, folding her close with the crook of his arm. Sliding his free hand over her shoulder blade, he tilted his head and kissed her. This was no my-sweet-friend kiss, no thoughtlessly affectionate kiss, no accidental or grateful kiss. This was about the woman who made him smile and want and forget. This was about not being able to help himself, about not even wanting to.

Lily relaxed against him, leaned against his chest and yielded her sweet lips to him. Her slender, finely boned hands stole up and over his shoulders to slip around his neck and into his hair. He smiled into that kiss, and she smiled, and he kissed her again.

He heard Isabella saying *Mama must like it in Heaven,* and he felt a new gladness. It was too much, too shocking. He broke the kiss and pressed his forehead to Lily's. The apples of her cheeks were as pink as roses, her smile so wide that he couldn't help smiling in return.

She had closed her fingers in the collar of his shirt and seemed to be having some trouble letting go, but her grip gradually loosened.

"I just thought you should know," he said, "that I had noticed."

Stepping back, he landed hard with one foot on

the stair below the small platform where they stood. They both laughed. He turned, went quickly down the stairs and out into the night, thankfully without falling on his face or breaking his neck. Spinning away from the door, he caught a clean breath.

He must be losing his mind. He should be keeping his distance and instead what did he do? He kissed her! Worse, he wanted... *God help me, I want Lily.*

Tate's thoughts stuttered to an abrupt halt.

Had he just reached out to God?

Yes, of course he had. And why not? He hadn't stopped believing any more than he'd stopped breathing. He'd just stopped reaching out, stopped daring to reach out.

He clapped a hand to the back of his neck and looked around him. He hadn't reached out to God in years, but Coraline and the mayor, Joe Sheridan, the Garmans and so many others had unashamedly hit their knees and asked for God's help in this time of trouble. And just look what had come of it.

An anonymous benefactor had stepped forward; as a result, downtown Bygones had transformed into a thing of beauty. The place hadn't looked this alive even when Randall's had been in operation. Main Street literally bustled these days. Oh, it didn't make up for Randall's closing, but it helped. It did. The community garden had helped, too, and what Lily had done this evening had helped. And they were just getting started!

Tate nodded and put his back to the painted brick beside the door. "Okay, God," he said. "Okay."

He still didn't get why Eve had to die, especially like that. Maybe he never would understand why that had to be. But he had to admit that, as Lily had said, sometimes things just worked out the way they should. That couldn't always be an accident, not when good people like her took the time to pray about them, not when folks pulled together and kept the faith, did kind things for one another and refused to quit. Maybe it was time he got over his loss, focused on his blessings, worked for—and expected—the best and took a few chances. Just look at what shy, retiring Lily had done, after all, bucking her whole family and moving halfway across the country to take a chance on a new home and an old dream. All in the hope of being noticed.

Well, he had noticed. Despite himself, despite his past, despite everything. And now he wanted her. He shouldn't, but he did.

Maybe, if things worked out between them, she would be as glad as he to forego a pregnancy. Not every woman felt the need to give birth to a child. She might be one of those women who liked kids and not babies or was willing to adopt or... He didn't dare hope for it. He didn't dare. But how did he not?

Chapter Eleven

The bike that Lily rode to the community garden on Friday morning was lavender in color. Knowing that she wouldn't sleep for thinking of that kiss, she'd stayed up Thursday evening to sand and paint the frame and fenders in the back of her shop, using cardboard to shield those parts that should remain unpainted. That morning before she'd left, she'd affixed a half-moon wicker hamper between the handlebars. She'd found the hamper at the This 'N' That and had thought to use it in a floral arrangement, but it worked perfectly as a basket for a lavender bicycle. She was a happy cyclist when she arrived just after dawn in tennis shoes, shorts and a snug T-shirt, her ponytail set off by the visor Tate had given her nearly a week earlier. Tate and several others were already on-site, including Josh Smith in his Cozy Cup Café van.

Kenneth met her with the news that he'd brought several small pots of herbs for her to sell at the flower shop. While she loaded these into her hamper, they discussed the possibility of his building strawberry wagons for her to sell. When that conversation concluded, she turned to find Tate ready with coffee and breakfast pastries for them to share.

"Josh says they're day-old," he reported, flicking crumbs from his shirt, "but they taste great to me."

Lily tried not to blush as she met his gaze, but she couldn't help it. No one had ever kissed her the way he had kissed her last night, as if she was Eve to his Adam. But then, he'd already had his Eve, and he'd told Lily in no uncertain terms that he didn't want another, so she would be foolish, indeed, to get her hopes up over a few kind words, a single dinner alone and a few expressions of affection. Tate was not the sort to lead a girl on or take advantage of her; it was much more likely that he'd felt sorry for her after her ill-advised confession on the trip back into town. She'd as good as told him that she'd never been kissed, not really kissed, anyway.

Besides, even if Tate should feel some real fondness for her, that didn't mean he was thinking about marriage, which brought other issues to mind. For one thing, he'd stated quite firmly that he wanted no more children and wouldn't go through another pregnancy. That was fine for him. He had Isabella, who was as adorable as could be, but Lily didn't think she could marry and not have a child of her own. She'd left Boston less because her sister had married a man she'd liked than because of her sister's stated intention to start a family right away. No, Lily didn't think she could give up the idea of a baby of her own, not even for Tate.

For another thing, she couldn't accept the idea of a Tate who didn't attend church and nursed a grudge against God. That, more than anything else, grieved her.

She took the coffee and pastry, trying not to think of anything else.

"Thank you."

"Don't thank me. Thank Josh Smith. And Melissa Sweeney."

They took a few moments to eat. Tate looked over her bike and pronounced it "sweet," grinning at the color and flipping the lid on the basket, mindful of the potted herbs inside.

"You never fail to amaze, Lily," he told her. She couldn't help wondering what that meant. Draining his coffee, he crumpled the cup and tossed it into the litter barrel nearby. Shaking his head, he muttered, "Lawyer," as he walked toward the garden.

She hurried to toss her half-eaten pastry and near-empty cup, catching up with him inside the fence. "What exactly do you mean by that?"

"You're too creative, kind-hearted and gentle to successfully practice law."

"That's a nice way of putting it," she returned wryly.

"Just the truth," Tate said.

The truth was that she'd been a terrible lawyer.

Her brother-in-law, before he *was* her brother-in-law, had once told her, after reviewing one of her briefs, that it was one thing to see both viewpoints in a lawsuit and another to *sympathize* too closely with both sides. He'd suggested, with some exasperation, that she might have a future in arbitration, but she hated confrontation too much to consider a career as a mediator.

Lily got busy. Danny and his friend Matt Garman seemed to make a point of working alongside her. Danny proved quite knowledgeable about the plants. Matt proved equally as well informed about the school.

"The teachers are all expecting layoff notices by the end of the first semester," he told her during the course of their conversation.

"That's awful," Lily said.

"We can still turn it around," Coraline insisted from two rows over. "We're planning fund-raisers, and if our tax base improves just a bit, we'll be okay."

"What about the police department, though?" Lily asked, straightening. "I heard they were worried about layoffs, too."

"More layoffs, you mean," someone said. "They've already cut to the bone."

"Yeah, and the Fire Department is all volunteer now," someone else said.

"Even the ambulance is staffed by volunteers from the clinic," Tate revealed.

"Man, Randall's plant closing down really hacked the heart out of this town," Kenneth muttered.

"No," Pastor Garman insisted, rising from a stooped position. "No, the heart of Bygones is strong. Look around you. This garden is evidence of that."

Murmurs of agreement went around the plot.

"The real trouble started when Randall's wife divorced him," someone said.

They all glanced around guiltily at that, as it smacked too much of gossip. Yet Lily sensed truth in the statement.

Wendy Garman sighed and said, "Divorce is a terrible thing, no matter how bad the marriage, but Hugh is right. The heart of Bygones is strong and vital. What we've done here, what the SOS Committee has done, what the newcomers have brought to us is all proof of that."

"I agree," Lily said, shaking off her work gloves.

Tate did the same and reached over to take her hand in his. "Me, too."

Coraline stripped off her gloves and grasped Tate's free hand. "Same here."

One by one the workers gathered around, linking hands there in the light of the rising sun, their feet planted among the rows and hillocks of the garden that the community had come together to make. Hugh Garman cleared his throat.

"Let us lay our hearts before God," he said quietly, bowing his head.

Lily watched as everyone present followed suit, including, after the slightest of hesitations, Tate. Lily felt rather than heard his gulp, and his hand tightened almost painfully on hers, but he joined the others as Hugh led the group in spontaneous prayer for their community. Hugh was brief but eloquent, asking for God's will to be done, for wisdom and guidance and blessing, for love and kindness to abound, for needs to be met and for their beloved little town to be saved if at all possible, before closing in the name of Christ Jesus. Amens wafted softly upon the morning air, and a sense of peace settled upon the garden.

Coraline gave Lily a beaming smile and hugged Tate, who seemed uncomfortable. Others also embraced. As Lily and Tate returned to work, Josh Smith came and pulled Coraline aside. Lily heard him ask if anything could be done about reopening the Randall plant. They went off to talk about it. If Tate seemed a bit troubled and withdrawn, Lily told herself that it was understandable.

To her mind, he fought a battle on two fronts now. He fought for Bygones and for his own spiritual health. She wasn't sure that he realized it yet, but she knew it and so did Coraline. She suspected that on some instinctive level even Isabella knew, and Lily suspected that God had used the crisis in Bygones to reach Tate, to show Tate that He was still active in the lives of His children. Lily prayed that, whatever happened, God wouldn't let Tate leave the field of battle until his personal war was won. She told herself that she would be happy with that. She just had to remember that Tate was not for her, no matter what her silly heart might say.

Now all she had to do was get through a birthday party without making a complete fool of herself over the man.

The hamster escaped midway into the party. One might think that an orange hamster in a miniature lime-green tutu would be easy to spot, even if it could nestle comfortably in the palm of an adult hand, but the dress-up box had been overturned and the girls had strewn boas, scarves and lacy shawls in all directions while outfitting themselves for tea. They loved playing dress-up, especially as they were allowed to put on play makeup and paint their nails, or rather, have their nails painted.

Lily did the actual painting, while Tate did his best to apply the teensy nail appliqués, peeling them from their paper backing with tweezers and placing them carefully on tiny wet fingernails. Often the fingers growing those nails were weighted with costume jewelry, enormous rings made of cheap paste and brilliant colors. The girls giggled, gestured wildly, called each other "dahling" while waiting for their nails to dry, and neglected the hamster because its silky fur stuck to their wet nail polish all too easily, hence the ease of its disappearance.

Ginny took advantage of the crisis to insist that

the girls clean up the mess they'd left behind them. Ten little girls in elaborate dress, toy high heels and party crowns, scurrying about and tossing leftover bits and baubles into, or at, a box, was as near complete chaos as Lily ever hoped to experience. Tate stood in the midst of it all, obviously afraid to move for fear of squashing something or someone, while Isabella choked back tears and repeatedly called, "Spunky!" as if the hamster would come to her.

Peter Bronson spied the little fellow, burrowing between the tan leather sofa cushions. In the short time that the small rodent had been missing, he had managed to chew a hole in a throw pillow and gnaw on the wood handle of a purse from the dress-up box. Tate consigned him to the safety of his habitat, which had taken pride of place on the coffee table in the living room. A relieved Ginny herded the girls into the dining room, where she had laid a lacy table with plastic dishes and a pretty bowl of floating roses, courtesy of Lily.

The girls could hardly wait to enjoy the luscious "cake" fashioned by the Sweet Dreams Bakery. Created of petit fours iced in pink-and-yellow fondant and decorated with delicate white flowers and elaborate letters, the individual cakes were placed in a checkerboard pattern that spelled out, Happy Eighth Birthday, Isabella! Tate lit the candles and everyone sang before Isabella blew out the candles in one great puff of breath, but then she asked to have them lit again so she could make a second wish. Tate shrugged and lit the candles again.

Isabella closed her eyes tight and blew out the candles once more. Everyone applauded. Ginny shook her head and began serving tiny sandwiches and cups of "punch tea," while Lily scooped ice cream and separated the little cakes onto plates. After a very giggly meal, Lily read a picture book about a tea party to the girls in Isabella's bedroom while Tate and Ginny set up several games in the living room and Peter started cleaning up after the tea party.

By the time the games were done, the girls had, of necessity, divested themselves of their costumes. Peter dutifully packed away the dress-up box, while Ginny put out small bags filled with party favors. Then they all sat down as Isabella opened her gifts. They were, as Tate had hoped, simple items having to do with the hamster: balls and wheels and a funny little swing, a mirror so Spunky could keep himself company, a hamster hat and hamster shoes and, best of all, a book about hamsters.

Isabella declared it "the best of all birthday parties ever."

The girls' parents proved prompt in picking them up, which was a good thing, as Peter seemed to have reached the end of his endurance.

"I am going home to take a nap," he announced, getting up off the sofa. He hugged his granddaughter and trudged out of the room.

"Lily," Ginny said, "I don't know what we would have done without you today."

"Oh, that's kind of you, ma'am. I enjoyed myself."

"Not as much as Isabella enjoyed you." She kissed Tate's cheek, hugged Isabella and followed her husband out.

"She's right," Tate said. "You were a huge help. Thank you."

"Thank you, Lily," Isabella echoed, hugging her.

"My pleasure entirely. By the way, I haven't given you my gift, yet."

Isabella drew back, her penciled eyebrows aloft. "Oh, boy, another gift!"

"It may not be what you're expecting," Lily said, moving around behind the easy chair where she'd stowed the gift bag. She brought the big pink bag forward and handed over a card that she'd bought at the grocery store. The card had a drawing of roses on the front but no verse inside, so Lily had hand-printed, "Roses for a little beauty. Happy birthday, Isabella. Love, Lily."

Isabella read the card aloud then delved into the bag and brought out a dark green plastic pot filled with dirt and several thorny sticks supporting tight green pods. Clearly puzzled, she blinked at Lily, who chuckled.

"It's a rosebush. It will have pink roses. Those are the buds."

Isabella gasped. "It'll grow roses?"

"That's right. Lots of them, or so Kenneth says.

It's not the very best time of the year to plant them, but I brought special soil and feed, and he says that if we follow the directions, this type should make lots and lots of roses by next spring. There's a little booklet in the bag telling all about it."

Isabella eagerly dug into the bag again and sat with Lily to go through the booklet, poring over the photos and directions.

"Will there be butterflies?" she asked breathlessly. "This photo shows butterflies."

"I suppose the blossoms will draw butterflies."

"Oh, I hope there'll be jillions of butterflies!"

Lily laughed. "That would be fun, wouldn't it?"

"It was one of my wishes," Isabella confessed softly. "I wished for butterflies."

Lily exchanged looks with Tate, who said, "I'll get a shovel and watering can. Why don't you let Lily help you wash your face and hands and meet me out back?"

Because the potting soil and plant food were in the bed of Tate's truck, that seemed like a good plan. He went out to the garage. Lily helped Isabella scrub off the play makeup and birthday cake, then they carried the rosebush and the booklet out the back door. Tate was ready with the shovel, having placed the watering can on the stoop.

"Let's take a look around," he said, "and decide where you want to plant your rosebush."

"I already know where I want to plant it," Isabella

announced. "Where I want the butterflies. At Mama's place."

Lily watched Tate's face drain of color and expression.

"Please, Daddy!" Isabella pleaded. "The flowers we leave there always die, and other people plant things, don't they?" He nodded jerkily. "Mama would see them when she looks down from Heaven," Isabella went on, "all the roses and the butterflies. She would like that, wouldn't she? Pink roses and butterflies?"

This wasn't at all what Lily had intended, but she couldn't very well intervene. The plan all along had been to allow Isabella to choose an appropriate spot for the rosebush. The last thing Lily wanted to do was remind Tate of his loss, but what spot could be more appropriate for Lily's rosebush than her mother's grave? All Lily could do was look away from the naked pain on Tate's face. He gulped and cleared his throat.

"Yes," he said thickly, "your mother would like that. Very much."

Isabella let out a happy sigh. "That was my first wish, butterflies for Mama." She grabbed Lily's hand. "Thank you, Lily. You gave me my wish!"

Lily managed a smile, but she could barely glance at Tate.

"You, uh, mind helping us do this?" he asked her. "Then I'll take you home."

Lily squeaked out, "I don't mind."

"Let's load up," he said tersely, snatching up the watering can.

Lily walked Isabella into the garage and helped her climb into the backseat of the truck. While Tate stowed the shovel and watering can in the bed of the pickup alongside the bags of potting soil and plant food, Lily belted Isabella into her seat and then did the same for herself. Isabella insisted on holding the rosebush in her lap. Tate slid behind the steering wheel, started the truck and backed it out of the garage.

They drove in silence to Bygones, turning west onto Church Street from Granary Road. Tate steered the truck past the church and on through town to a shady glen about a half-mile outside the city limits. The wrought-iron gate that arched over the graveled road into the cemetery gave two establishment dates, 1870 and 1970. Lily surmised that the cemetery had been moved from its original site, probably next door to the church, to this beautiful place when it had outgrown its space in town.

Eve's grave lay on a small rise, marked at one end by a pink granite bench and on the other by a matching headstone, identifying her as a beloved wife and mother who had left this life too soon. Isabella read her booklet and picked the south side of her mother's headstone for the rosebush. Grimly Tate dug the hole to the required specifications. Lily opened the plant food and dumped it into the hole, then covered it with the prepackaged soil. Together

Tate and Isabella gently removed the bush, dirt and all, from the pot. They placed the entire thing into the ground, covered the lump of dirt with more of the potting soil and then with soil that Tate had dug out of the hole. While Lily and Isabella gently packed the soil around the plant, Tate went to a hydrant and filled the watering can, then he came back and helped Isabella water the ground all around the bush.

"We have to come back every day and water it unless it rains," Isabella told him.

"We will," he promised.

Father and daughter stood side by side and stared at their handiwork for a long time, while Lily stood next to the bench and silently prayed that the bush would flourish with so many blooms that the canes would bow before the heavens and butterflies would paint the skies.

"A wish is like a prayer when you say it to God, isn't it?" Isabella asked softly. No one answered her, but she didn't seem to require an answer. She looked up at her father then and said, "I have another wish. Remember?" Tate looked down at her, and she softly said, "I wished my daddy would go to church with me on my birthday."

Lily reeled back a step, but Tate did not move a hair for the longest time. Then suddenly he turned and strode for the truck, bending to snatch up the shovel and watering can in mid stride. Isabella ran to Lily and clasped her hand.

"It's not really my birthday yet," she said hopefully, so obviously seeking reassurance that Lily could have wept. In fact, Lily felt perilously close to tears.

"Sweetie," she said, sitting down on the bench, "God is not Santa Claus. He does answer our prayers, depending on what is best for us. Sometimes He says Yes, and sometimes, No, and sometimes, He just wants us to wait for a while. Sometimes, though, what we want depends on someone else, someone other than God. In that case, free will applies. You see, God won't make any of us do what we don't want to do, even if we should do it and it's good for us. He might make us awfully miserable for not doing it, but He'll wait for us to do the right thing."

"But Daddy makes me do stuff I don't want to do 'cause it's good for me."

"I know, but you're a child. Your grandma and grandpa don't make your daddy do things now that he's an adult, do they?"

Isabella had to think about it. Finally, she shook her head. "No-o-o."

"Well, God is like that. He gives us every chance to do what is right and best on our own, to teach us and lead us, but ultimately, we choose our behavior. Understand?"

Isabella looked to the truck where her father waited. The doors stood open, and the shovel and watering can had been stowed. He stood next to the driver's door, arms folded, head bowed.

"I think so," she whispered.

Lily hugged her. "You made good wishes. You must have been thinking about how to please your Mommy for a while now." Isabella nodded.

"Grandma says Mama watches us from Heaven."

"I believe that's so."

"Well, I can't give her gifts on her birthday, so I tried to think of something else."

"You see, God knew that," Lily told her, tapping her on the tip of her nose, "and He put the idea of the rosebush into my mind so He could answer your wish when you made it. Now He's working on your daddy's heart. One day, I'm sure, your daddy will go to church again. Just don't be too disappointed if it's not tomorrow."

"Grandma says he's still getting over Mama dying."

"I'm sure she's right about that."

Isabella sighed. "I guess 'cause I don't remember her I got over it already."

"But you still think of her," Lily said, getting to her feet. "That's what counts."

Isabella nodded, walked over to the discarded plastic pot and picked it up. "One wish out of two is good," Isabella remarked happily.

Lily smiled and put out her hand. "Very good."

Isabella put her hand in Lily's, and they headed for the truck.

"Besides, I got lots of cool stuff for Spunky."

"You did, and we had lots of fun, too, didn't we?"

They were laughing about something that happened in one of the games when they got to the truck. Tate seemed more relaxed. He shot Lily a look of gratitude, but he let her boost Isabella up into her seat again.

When he stopped the truck in front of her apartment a few minutes later, he thanked her once more for her help that day. Lily proclaimed that she'd had a lovely time then let herself out of the truck. It all felt very proper, sadly distant and impersonal. He drove away and left her standing there on the sidewalk, wondering if she would ever see him or Isabella again.

Oh, they would meet on the street and at the garden from time to time. She would see them around town and, in Isabella's case, at least, in church, but after today, Lily doubted if she would ever again receive a private invitation from or a personal meeting with Tate Bronson. She had unwittingly gotten too close. She had unintentionally invaded the space belonging to his beloved Eve. She had accompanied him and his daughter to his late wife's graveside. How much more invasive and cloying could she get?

No, she couldn't have driven him away more effectively if she had tried, but what did it matter? She already knew that he was not for her, and she had the consolation of Isabella's determination to get her dad back into church. Lily would pray toward that end, and meanwhile, she would take heed of her own lesson.

She would choose the behaviors that were good and right, trusting God to lead and inform her. She would do her best here in Bygones, and trust Him with the outcome. Everyone else would do what he or she would, but Lily would pray and choose obedience and simply trust for the best.

Chapter Twelve

Tate's mother made sandwiches for dinner, saving the big meal for Isabella's actual birthday the next day. She and Isabella talked happily about the birthday party that afternoon, and Peter polished off two big sandwiches and a mountain of potato chips, along with a mammoth chunk of watermelon, while Tate nibbled and pretended to participate. In reality Isabella's wishes and Lily's part in them circled through his mind, blunting his hearing and clogging his speech.

To his surprise, Isabella said nothing to her grandparents of the rosebush or her desire to have him attend church with her the next day, but Tate's mind was so full of those things that he knew his parents must sense something. Eventually Isabella would spill the beans, of course, but he couldn't really think of that. He couldn't really think at all. He was too full of feeling, too stuffed with fullness, with parenthood and spirituality and life itself, with

Lily and his daughter, with the past and the present and the future. It was as if his world had exploded. All the pieces were still there, but they hadn't settled into the right places, and he didn't know where to begin or how to fit them back together again.

Finally he just couldn't pretend to pay attention anymore, so he got up from his mother's table and said, "I need to go."

She didn't question him. Instead she simply asked if it wouldn't be best if Isabella stayed the night.

"I think it might," he said, surprising them all, himself included. "I'll bring clothes over for her in the morning."

"Will you feed Spunky?" Isabella asked in a small voice.

Tate bent and kissed her on the top of the head. "I promise."

She wrapped her arms around his waist. "Good night, Daddy."

"Good night. I love you."

"Love you, too."

He left quickly, relieved to go and, for once, to leave his daughter behind. What had she talked about with Lily, he wondered, there at her mother's graveside? At the same time he wasn't sure that he wanted to know.

For some reason he couldn't go home, at least not then. Instead he drove around aimlessly for what felt like hours, until he realized that all along he had been headed back to the cemetery. He parked exactly where he'd parked earlier that day, and he walked out to the grave with his hands in his pockets, his boots scuffing against the ground. When he got to the bench, he sat down.

Leaning forward, he rubbed his hands over his face. The moon hung low over the horizon, waning but very nearly full, a great pale orb against the charcoal velvet of the sky, smudged at the top by the wispy suggestion of a cloud. He didn't know why he had come. Eve was not here. Her corpse lay in an ornate box beneath his feet, but Eve was not here. He had never felt that she might be here, never pretended that she might be, never sought comfort at this place. This, as he had told his daughter, was a place of remembrance, nothing more, so he remembered.

He remembered the laughing girl who had worried that her teeth were too big and that his mother didn't like her. He remembered how she'd made him feel as if he were the solution to all her problems, the center of her world. He remembered how that had subtly shifted after they had married. Their home and then her pregnancy and finally her faith had taken center stage in her life. He had gone from her knight in shining armor to the husband who worked too many hours and left her alone too much.

He pictured the rosebush, growing wild and untamed, heavy with pink blossoms, butterflies flitting about them. Eve would love that as much as Isabella. Eve would want him to go to church, too.

Eve would want him and their daughter to be happy. Eve would not want him to be alone and angry.

Eve, who had loved him and wanted to be a mother. Eve, who had thought he worked too much and had too much to prove and took things too seriously. Eve, whose cooking had left a lot to be desired, and who had wanted to live in town and worried that they were too far from the hospital. Eve, who had laughed so often and cried so easily. Eve, his high school sweetheart and first love but perhaps not his only love, forever young while he would grow older and hopefully wiser.

He thought of all the things he had said he would never do. He would never forgive. He would never understand. He would never forget. He would never go back. He would never love again, never risk the kind of loss and pain he'd already suffered.

"I don't understand," he said aloud. He still couldn't make any sense of what had happened. What possible purpose could Eve's death serve? How could God let it happen like that, so suddenly and swiftly on the very day of their daughter's birth? "I can't forget."

As for the rest…maybe he could take some risk. He didn't have to risk *all,* but *some* risk might be acceptable.

He got up and looked around him. It was peaceful and lovely here, a good place.

"I love you, Evie, but I know you're in Heaven

and that you like it there. I hope you like your butterflies. Goodbye."

He remembered how he used to drive by Eve's grandmother's house when they were in school. Her parents were killed in a trucking accident when Eve was small, then old Mrs. Hoyt had died during Eve's senior year in high school. Eve had lived with friends until she'd graduated and they had married. Tate used to drive by at night, and she'd wave to him from the window. He walked back to the truck and drove away, ready for home and bed.

Pink roses and daisies were not a combination that Lily often used, but something about them, when mixed with baby's breath and ivy, just sang Isabella to her, so that was what she chose for the white patent leather handbag that graced the altar that Sunday morning. They made a very pretty display atop the grass-green runner bisecting the top of the carved wood altar. Lily had signed the list and provided the flower arrangement herself, though Ginny Bronson had come into the shop and offered to do it the very day after Lily had penciled in her name. Lily had done it because she'd wanted to choose the flowers, though at the time she hadn't known what she would choose to go with the pink roses. The rest had come to her after she'd decided on the container, as was often the case. Something about that prissy little handbag said Isabella.

Miss Mars, who had again provided the inspiration, was beside herself with pride. "I had one just like that in 1965 and the shoes to match!" she gushed from the pew on Lily's left that Sunday morning.

"Didn't we all?" asked Coraline, who sat next to Miss Mars.

Lily glanced at the bottom of the printed program, where it was announced, in italics, *"Today's altar flowers are given in honor of Miss Isabella Bronson's eighth birthday."* Lily hoped Isabella would be pleased, that the flowers would be enough to make up for any disappointment she might suffer due to an unfulfilled second birthday wish. Who'd ever heard of a second birthday wish, anyway? Lily was quite prepared to say as much if the girl should turn up gloomy. She'd taken a seat at the end of the row so she would be sure to spot the girl and her grandparents when they came in.

Even as that thought presented itself, a murmur of voices and flurry of activity had her turning her head to the right. Suddenly Isabella was there, hugging Lily's neck and whispering loudly, "It's my wish, Lily! It's my wish!"

Lily felt herself nudged none-too-gently, both elbows and knees prodding her. Miss Mars, tittering like a cuckoo, shifted down the pew, so Lily did the same, Isabella in tow, still talking.

"And the flowers. They're so beautiful! Grandma said you did 'em all on your own. Thank you. Thank you." This last was punctuated with noisy kisses that snapped Lily's head back.

"All right, all right. We're making quite enough of a scene already."

The sound of Tate's chuckling voice sent Lily's jaw to her knees. She batted at Isabella's riotous curls and finally disengaged the exuberant child's arms to settle the little one into the pew so she could gape past her red head.

"Good morning, Ms. Farnsworth," Tate said, reaching past his daughter to curl a finger beneath Lily's chin and gently close her mouth for her.

"You're here," she declared stupidly, staring at him in his gray suit.

Isabella slid her hand into Lily's and lifted her feet onto the edge of the pew, avidly watching the byplay between the adults. Tate calmly brushed Isabella's Mary Janes down again.

"So I am." He grinned, and tapped Lily on the end of the nose. "So are you."

Lily burbled with laughter, unaware that tears rolled down her cheeks until a tsking Tate dropped a folded handkerchief into her lap. Using her free hand, she picked it up and dabbed at her cheeks. The pianist began to play just then, and the music leader stepped up to ask the congregation to stand for the opening hymn. Tate reached out to take Lily's arm, lifting both her and Isabella with him as he rose. When he reached down for the hymnal, she leaned forward at the same time as Ginny and

Peter Bronson. Their gazes met across the aisle, and they nodded to Lily, as if giving her credit for the phenomenon sitting next to their granddaughter.

A lump in her throat, Lily gave her head a little shake. She hadn't done this. Tate wasn't here for her. This was Isabella's doing, Isabella's and God's. Surely Isabella had told them so. Looking to her left, Lily traded teary smiles with Miss Mars and Coraline.

Her mind awhirl, Lily faced the altar. Behind it an arch framed a tall cross of rough wood. The stained glass of the narrow upper row of sanctuary windows cast rays of color across the room, creating a prism of color of the morning light around the cross. That old wood cross had never looked so lovely to Lily. It had never carried such meaning for her. The God of salvation and love answered prayers, even when they came in the form of a little girl's birthday wish.

As the voices of the congregation lifted in a song of praise, Lily lifted a silent prayer of thanksgiving to the Almighty.

Tate had known, of course, that it wouldn't be as simple as showing up in a suit and parking his behind on a pew. The light gray suit was the same one that he'd worn to his sister's wedding over three years ago. He'd been surprised to find that it fit a bit too snugly across the chest and in the upper arms. It would do for today, but he'd have to plan a trip to purchase a replacement. A man shouldn't be

without a good suit, after all, especially as he had
no doubt that regular church attendance was once
again in his future.

Strangely he didn't mind. Just the opposite. It was
time, time to come home.

Things had changed, and nothing had changed.
Instead of making announcements at the beginning
of the service, as they had used to do, they began
with a congregational song, saving the announcements for last, according to the bulletin. Other elements of the service had also been juggled, but all
were familiar.

Tate had missed singing. He hadn't realized it
until he'd opened the hymnal and actually started
to sing, but he'd missed the feeling of lifting his
voice, especially in concert with others. He wasn't
the best singer or the worst, but he could carry a
tune, and singing with others seemed to make him
better. Something more happened, however. He realized that he had a need to praise God, not just to
sing about Him but a need to actually praise Him,
to worship.

He remembered a time when he had foolishly told
himself that he would never be able to truly worship
again. He'd told himself that his doubts, anger, disappointment and grief would forever taint his rev-
erence for the Almighty. Somehow, over time, that
had all changed, however. Without him even realizing it, his hunger for God had slowly and quietly
grown until even his anger could not stand against

it. In the end, a little girl's "second birthday wish" had been all it had taken to overcome that.

The service proved somewhat troubling merely because Tate had some difficulty with concentration. Perhaps he was out of practice, or perhaps the problem was Lily sitting just an arm's length away there on the other side of Isabella, looking pretty in a straight sleeveless dress of peach-colored lace with a big square collar that overlapped her slender shoulders. Whatever the reason, he found his thoughts wandering after the Scripture reading, which came from the third chapter of Second Timothy.

His mind snagged on the sixteenth and seventeenth verses: *All Scripture is given by inspiration of God, and is profitable for doctrine, for reproof, for correction, for instruction in righteousness: that the man of God may be complete, thoroughly equipped for every good work.*

That word *complete* jumped out at him. He hadn't felt complete since Eve's death. Or maybe the truth was that he'd felt even *less* complete after Eve had died. She'd always said that he'd seemed to have something to prove because everyone thought they'd married too young, and maybe that had been true. At times he'd felt that she was the only one on his side, and then suddenly she'd been gone, leaving him a single father. Maybe that was why he'd pored over his Bible in those dark days that had followed her passing. He'd needed answers for her death, so he'd dug through books like Lamentations and

Psalms, Ecclesiastes, James and even Revelation. He hadn't found the answers that he'd sought, and he'd refused to come to church until he had. He realized now, in the back of his mind, he'd felt that he was punishing God by staying at home on Sunday mornings, but he'd really been hurting himself. And his daughter.

The joy on Isabella's face this morning had been eclipsed only by her sobs when she'd leaped into his arms and wept upon realizing why he'd shown up wearing a suit. That had humbled him as nothing else could have done, so he would make a concerted effort to leave the past behind and go forward. He wanted completion, and God knew that he hadn't found it on his own.

After the service, which seemed surprisingly short, people seemed torn between knocking him senseless by pounding his back in welcome and playing it cool, as if they saw him there every Sunday. Tate felt happy with either reaction. He just felt happy, period. It was weird. His insides quivered like the proverbial bowlful of jelly, but the sun seemed to shine a little brighter—on what was turning out to be an overcast day—and he found himself grinning like an idiot when no reason could be found for it, except…well, maybe returning to church had been easier than he'd expected, after all. He'd thought he'd have moments of unease, at least, but he really hadn't.

It had been a lot like walking back into the school

the day when he'd enrolled Isabella for preschool or that day Coraline had called everyone to the principal's office to start the SOS Committee. In each case years had passed since he'd last walked through those specific doors, but he'd felt just as at home as ever.

"So," Lily asked, as soon as they had a moment to themselves, Isabella having run off to speak to her grandparents, "was it as difficult as you expected?"

Tate couldn't help himself; he burst out laughing. "No," he managed. "It wasn't. Not at all." He sobered to a grin. "In fact, it was quite enjoyable."

"Then what was so funny?" she asked, chuckling uncertainly, her wary gaze casting about them in little jerks of concern.

"Well, lightning didn't strike, for one thing."

Her blue eyes zipped to his face. "Tate!"

"I'm joking. I'm joking. It's just that I had it built up in my mind as this earth-shattering event and, well, it turns out to be pretty much like the last time I was here."

"I guess that's good," she said hopefully, rocking from heel to toe and toe to heel.

"I think so."

He wasn't the least surprised when his mother approached then to invite Lily to come over for Sunday dinner. "It being Isabella's actual birthday, and especially after all the help you gave us at the party yesterday."

Tate had no doubt that the matchmaking little

miss had instigated the whole thing, not that he minded really, though he would have to be careful not to inflame his daughter's all-too-active imagination. He wasn't sure where all this was going. Lily was, first and foremost, Isabella's friend, and he didn't know that she would ever be more than that. Yes, he had finally said goodbye to Eve, and he was finally back in church and glad to be talking to God again. Plus, he liked Lily. In truth, he more than liked Lily. Still, he'd learned some hard lessons in life, and he wasn't about to forget them.

Lily ducked her head, delicate color rising to her cheeks. Her eyes skittered behind the lenses of her glasses, her innate shyness reasserting itself. He thought for a moment that she would refuse his mother's invitation, but then she lifted her chin, smiled and nodded her head.

"Thank you," she said softly. "That would be lovely."

"Let everyone get changed," his mother instructed Tate smartly, "then bring Lily and Isabella along. Your father wants to eat before the baseball game starts."

"Not much hope of that," Tate warned.

"That's what I told him."

"We'll be as quick as we can."

"That's all I ask." His mom went off to join her impatiently gesturing husband.

Tate looked to Lily then. "So how do you want to do this?"

"Just drop me at the apartment and give me three minutes."

He chuckled. Eve used to say three minutes when she meant thirty. With Lily three minutes probably meant ten. He'd give her the ten happily. Then they'd head out to his place so he and Isabella could swap their Sunday best for family comfortable before going over to his parents' house.

Lily excused herself briefly to apprise Coraline and Miss Mars of the situation. By the time she rejoined them, Tate had belted his daughter into her seat in the truck, warned her to be on her best behavior, and held an open door for Lily.

She smiled at him as he handed her up into the cab of the truck, and he instantly remembered kissing her. Suddenly he wondered if having her over for the afternoon was such a good idea. He seemed to lose his head with Lily. She'd wormed her way into his heart with surprising speed. In her own quiet, unassuming way, Lily Farnsworth was a dangerous woman.

Still, what was he going to do? Tell her that he'd changed his mind and was rescinding his mother's dinner invitation? He was surely man enough to behave with good sense and some measure of discipline.

He dropped her at the apartment as suggested and waited in the truck at the curb. Lily proved that she could tell time while changing her clothes better than the average woman of his acquaintance.

She skipped back down the stairs in under five minutes, wearing hay-colored cotton capris and a matching top embroidered with turquoise-blue hummingbirds. On her feet were turquoise-blue sandals with enough sparkle to make Isabella sit up and take notice.

She jabbered delightedly about getting a pair for herself all the way out to the ranch. Once there she had to be bullied up to her room, and only Lily could coax her into suitable clothing for a casual afternoon at her grandparents' house. She wanted to dress up as she had for the tea party the previous day, but Lily convinced her, before Tate could lose his temper, that was not a good idea. Tate put his foot down about bringing Spunky along with them, however, pointing out that Grandpa's dog and Grandma's cat would not appreciate Spunky's presence.

"Besides," as he told Lily, "I know it's her birthday, but she can't have *everything* she wants."

"I didn't say she should."

"Uh-huh, but I know that look."

He wondered if that look could mean that Isabella was enough for her, then chastised himself for wondering.

By the time they finally piled into the truck and sped off to his parents' place, Tate knew that his dad was going to have to interrupt his ball game to eat, but Tate did his best, as promised, throwing up dust getting over there. As he pushed through the screen door into his mother's kitchen, he could hear the TV in the other room.

"Ball game's on, huh?"

"He's waiting for you to set the DVR so he won't miss anything."

"I better get in there." His dad had a way of messing up the DVR settings, but Tate couldn't help feeling that he was abandoning Lily. Still, she wasn't *his* guest. *He* hadn't invited her. He was just the transportation.

Besides, if she was Eve, he wouldn't think twice about leaving her with his mom. Nevertheless, walking out of that room required a surprising amount of steel. *Staying* out of it proved to be one of the most difficult things he'd ever done.

Chapter Thirteen

Ginny had a way of drawing Lily into the work of meal preparation without making her feel awkward about it. Isabella sat at the kitchen table and colored in a stack of well-used coloring books. This was apparently a favorite activity at her grandmother's house, but Lily didn't believe for a moment that her little ears weren't pricked for every sound and nuance of what passed between the two women as they moved about the small, dated kitchen.

The elder Bronsons' house had little in common with that of their son. Though two-story and wrapped-in porches, it was much smaller, older and had been sided entirely in clapboard, which could use a good wash and a coat of white paint. Yet it exuded an aura of home and warmth. The older appliances, olive green in color, gleamed with cleanliness, as did the white tile floor and countertops. The yellow walls behind the olive green cabinets showed off decades' worth of handprints in clay disks, Bible verses printed on cardboard and decorated with colored macaroni, bird feathers shellacked to bits of wood and designs glued to strips of felt. These were the keepsakes of childhood, the sort of things Lily's own mother had displayed on her desk for a prescribed period of time and then relegated to a special box until the end of each school year, when two special keepsakes would be chosen. Lily liked that Ginny Bronson still kept the offerings of her own children as decorations in the heart of her home.

She saw framed colorings of Isabella's, too. The old-fashioned refrigerator was plastered with them. Lily couldn't help wondering where Tate kept Isabella's bits of artwork. She'd seen some things on his nice big stainless steel fridge but only a few. Maybe Isabella was prone to gifting her grandmother with her artwork. Then again, she'd given Lily quite a number of her colorings. Lily put the matter out of mind to help carry food to the table in the other room as Ginny dished up the meal.

Because the dining room was in one end of the long narrow living area, Ginny had an iron-clad rule about the television not being on during mealtime, so Peter and Tate dutifully shut off the set and came to the maple table. Peter took the chair at one end of the long oval. Tate chose a chair in the center, leaving the seat at the other end for Ginny. Isabella sat across from her father, and Ginny had laid an extra place beside her for Lily.

The china, Ginny had told Lily, had once be-
longed to Peter's grandmother. Many of the serving pieces were as cobwebbed and darkened as the
ivy-latticed dinnerware, but that seemed appropriate
when piled high with fried chicken, mashed potatoes, green beans and cream gravy—all Isabella's
favorites, which she mentioned while giving thanks
for the food.

"Not that her grandmother spoils her or anything," Tate said pointedly, following the prayer.

"And not that you don't benefit significantly from
that," Lily observed as he loaded his plate.

"Hey, I won't get fed like this again until my own
birthday," he objected.

"Which isn't so far away," Lily remarked un-
thinkingly. "September, isn't it?"

"The sixth," Isabella confirmed, reaching for a
buttered roll.

Lily pushed the bread basket a little closer to her,
but she still caught the look that passed between
Ginny and Peter, as if they found significance in
her knowing the month of Tate's birth. She bit her
lip, trying to think of a way to explain that Isabella
had told her both her father's birth date and his age
within the first hour of their meeting. Abandoning
the effort, she asked Tate what he would choose for
his own birthday dinner.

Ginny and Peter both laughed.

"Catfish," Isabella supplied. "Fried catfish."

"With corn bread, cole slaw, and potatoes cooked

up with onions, celery and peppers," Tate said, shaking his fork at his mother.

"As if I'm likely to forget," she said to Lily. "He's been eating the same birthday dinner since he was twelve."

"Remember the year Eve tried to bake the catfish?" Peter asked with a chortle.

Everyone at the table froze.

A trio of heartbeats later, Tate finished chewing and swallowed then looked at Lily, a half smile curling one corner of his lips. "Nearly put me off catfish for good," he said easily before switching his attention back to his plate. He forked up a bite of potatoes and gravy. "She was just trying to 'healthy things up,' as Dad puts it." He smiled to himself, adding, "But the good Lord intended catfish to be fried. Period." He ate the potatoes, following them with green beans, and said no more.

"Sadly, too many of our favorite things are fried," Ginny put in, obviously trying to change the subject.

"That's why we only eat them on special occasions," Peter added, biting into a chicken leg.

"We've still got birthday cake!" Isabella reminded everyone brightly.

"Which you don't get unless you eat every green bean on your plate," Tate reminded her.

Everyone laughed as she started scooping in the green veggies.

The mood once again normalized, Lily relaxed and let herself soak up the warm family atmosphere.

She loved her family, but she was glad not to have to discuss torts and dialectics at the dinner table, let alone politics and jurisprudence. She had never fared well in those discourses, for she didn't care to raise her voice or approach every conversation as a debate. It was nice to sit down to dinner with people who simply enjoyed each other's company rather than felt they had to pick sides in an argument. She'd relaxed at dinner with her friends, of course, but this felt different, almost like dining with her own family, which was a very dangerous thought, indeed, as dangerous as Tate Bronson himself.

She tried to focus on Isabella. She was here because of Isabella, after all.

Now, if only she could manage not to fall in love with Isabella's father.

She had promised herself that she would be satisfied with getting him back into church, after all, and she meant to stick to that. This time she wasn't going to play the fool. This time she was going to guard her heart and be very wise—if it wasn't already too late.

"Thanks, Mom," Tate said, rising from the table with both belly and heart feeling that they were about to burst. "Great meal. As always."

Normally he and his father would help clear the table before going back to the game, but with Lily there already gathering up dishes, he didn't dare offer to help. He'd eaten far too much just to stay at the table with her. The last thing he ought to do was follow her into the kitchen where she'd be within easy reach, especially with his eagle-eyed mother there, pretending not to notice their every move while cataloging each nuance of their interaction. Instead he pointed at Isabella.

"The birthday celebrations are officially at an end, young lady. Now you are on dish detail."

"Da-a-ad."

"I mean it."

"But what about my cake?"

"Later."

Isabella sighed and climbed down off her chair. "Oh, all right." She couldn't possibly be hungry anyway. Like him, she'd eaten far more than her fair share.

Lily shot him an amused glance as Isabella grabbed the empty bread basket and started toward the kitchen.

"You're trailing bread crumbs," her grandmother admonished mildly, following along after her with a stack of plates.

"I'll get the sweeper!" Isabella cried, breaking into a run.

For some reason she loved the old manual sweeper that his mother kept in the pantry. She'd run the thing back and forth over the floor for hours. At least it didn't make enough racket to interfere with the television. Shaking his head, Tate made his way to the sofa and collapsed. Peter came right behind him, taking his usual place in the recliner, and picked up the remote.

Tate soon had to take over. Try as he might, Peter could not seem to get the hang of the DVR system. Left to his own devices, he'd miss half the game or, at best, manage to pick up where they'd left off, only to settle for watching the rest of the program along with all of the commercials, breaks and replays. Tate soon had them caught up to the game in real time without missing any of the actual action. All the while he was aware of the hum of conversation and activity coming from the kitchen, especially the laughter. Especially Lily's laughter.

Like everything else about Lily, her laughter had an ethereal quality to it, an airy, delicate lilt. He analyzed the sound in his mind: husky and whispery, yet tinkling, as if a gossamer veil overlay a crystal chime.

His father whooped as the Royals batted in a double play, calling Tate's attention back to the game. Tate sat up straight and rubbed a hand over his face. The woman would reduce him to poetry if he wasn't careful. He forced himself to concentrate.

After a while, his mother, daughter and Lily came in to join the men. His mother took her usual place in the easy chair. Isabella went to her knees in front of the coffee table to color and work through picture mazes, leaving Lily to squeeze into the corner of the sofa opposite him. She needn't have *squeezed,* of course. The sofa was quite long enough for him to stretch out full-length, but she seemed to feel that she needed to get as far away from him as humanly possible while still occupying the same piece of furniture.

For some reason that irritated Tate. He found himself sprawling all over the place, trying to close the distance, which just caused her to draw up tighter. Disgusted with himself, he got up to get a glass of iced tea.

"Anyone else want a drink?"

He hoped that everyone would want something so Lily would have to help him or that Lily would want her own and follow him into the kitchen to get it. Unfortunately he seemed to be the only one thirsty. Taking himself off to the kitchen, he slammed around getting ice into a glass and tea poured over it. Carrying the tumbler back into the living room, he sat himself down again—in the corner opposite Lily.

Before long Isabella crawled up onto the sofa between them. She put her head in Lily's lap and her feet in Tate's and proceeded to sing quietly to herself. Lily, who didn't seem to have much interest in baseball, bowed her head over Isabella's, her long pale hair creating a wavy curtain around them, and just as quietly sang along. The two of them giggled, and Lily playfully shushed Isabella before they started in on a second song.

Tate couldn't help smiling at them. When he looked up, he caught his mother watching him watch Lily and Isabella. She quickly looked down at the magazine she had opened on her lap, but her small, knowing smile stayed in place. He mentally recalled some of the things he'd said to his mother about this woman.

Lily? Oh, Isabella is particularly taken with her, and since I'm her SOS Committee contact, she's naturally going to be around at times.

I kind of feel sorry for that Lily Farnsworth. She's shy, doesn't make friends easily, and since I'm her official SOS host I feel we ought to include her in what we can.

The town owes a lot to the newcomers, you know, especially that Lily Farnsworth, and she's been so patient with Isabella that I feel sort of responsible for her.

He wondered if his mom understood his interest in Lily, then mentally snorted. She'd probably seen it before he had. Ginny had always been clear-eyed about things. She'd seen that him and Eve marrying so young had been as much about Eve's living situation as about their feelings for each other. His parents had wanted him to go to college after high school like his older sister, but Eve hadn't had that option. The friend with whose family Eve had lived after her grandmother's death had been all set to go off to college herself, which meant that Eve needed a new situation, but she couldn't support herself working part-time at the grocery store, and she didn't want to leave Bygones and any chance of being with him. The only solution had been to marry and make a home together. Ginny had supported his decision. She hadn't liked it, but she'd understood it. He'd gone to college online and long distance, making the drive to and from Manhattan twice weekly while working full-time on the farm, building his own house and doing his best to prove that the decision to marry had been right.

Eve had felt neglected, and he hadn't even seen it until his mother had pointed it out to him. That was when they'd decided to have a baby. Eve had been talking about it for a while, but he'd been focused on other things. Suddenly it had seemed like a good idea. Eve would have a baby upon whom to focus her attention, and he could take care of his business without worrying that she felt lonely, and he'd liked the idea of being a dad.

The amazing thing was how blind he'd continued to be after Eve's death. He'd refused to see that staying out of church was hurting everyone around him but God, himself included, while all along God had been patiently waiting for him to wise up and come home. He'd focused on his own pain and loss, to the exclusion of everything and everyone outside his own immediate family, until the whole town had been threatened with extinction. Even then, it had taken a little girl's second birthday wish and a shy, sweet woman with a pink rosebush to make him see what he needed to do and where he needed to be. The question was, where did he go from here?

It was a question he'd tried to avoid, but it suddenly gnawed at him, wouldn't leave him alone. He could barely keep from squirming.

His dad erupted with a cheer, throwing himself forward in his chair and howling at the TV. "Run, run! Slide in there. Safe! Yahoo!"

"Your father's whole day is made," Ginny quipped, waving a hand at Tate. "The Royals go into the ninth inning four runs ahead."

"That's enough of a breather for me," Tate declared, on the edge of his seat. "How about you, Lily?"

Her head came up. "I beg your pardon?"

"You interested in watching the rest of this game?"

She glanced around, blinking as if just becoming aware of her surroundings. "Uh, I'm not much of a baseball aficionado."

"So you don't mind missing the rest of the game?"

"No."

"Great. Let's go then."

"Oh. Okay."

Lily helped Isabella sit up then rose to her feet. Isabella bounced onto her feet, too.

"Not you," Tate instructed, waving Isabella back. "You're staying here."

"Why can't I come?"

"Because I said so."

"But—"

"You want your cake, don't you?" her grand-mother asked quickly.

Isabella's eyes lit up. "Yum." She dropped back down onto the sofa.

Tate grabbed Lily's hand and hauled her out of there before he could think better of what he was doing. He didn't want to think about it, didn't want to analyze it. He was taking a chance, but so be it. Things would either work out or they wouldn't.

"Thank you for dinner," she called to his par-ents as he dragged her from the room. "I enjoyed myself."

"You're welcome," Ginny called after her.

"Come anytime!" Peter yelled.

"Bye, Lily!"

"Bye, Isabella. See you soon."

Tate pushed through the kitchen door and out onto the porch. They were halfway to the truck when Lily asked, "What's the hurry?"

He stopped where he was and turned to face her. "No hurry. No hurry at all. I just thought we'd go for a drive before the sun sets."

"Oh. That sounds like fun."

"Yeah," he said, surprised, given that the idea had just occurred to him. "You haven't had a chance to see much around here, have you?"

"No, I haven't."

"Good. Then I'll show you around."

"Great."

They loaded up and set out. For almost two hours

they drove around the countryside, first around the Bronson acreage, all two thousand of them—or as many as could be reached by vehicle. Then they set out to explore the remaining compass points. He showed her the Happy Havens Animal Shelter, various farms and ranches, the little country chapel tucked into a pretty dale, the lovely old bridge built over a babbling creek, everything he could think of that might interest her.

"This land isn't as flat and featureless as I first thought it was," Lily said after a while. That surprised Tate. He wasn't sure why, really. The plains of Kansas had long been stereotyped exactly as she'd described them. Having lived here his whole life, however, he'd always known their intricacies. Some part of him had assumed that Lily recognized their subtle beauty, too. And perhaps she did.

As they drove, the sky darkened to solider blue, the clouds at last scudding away, their underbellies painted with fiery reds and oranges as the sun sank below the horizon. The blue gradually gave way completely to gray and gray to black liberally sprinkled with diamond-bright stars and a three-quarter moon that hung so low he could almost reach out and touch it.

"We don't have stars like this in Boston," she said dreamily when he turned the truck at last for town.

He chuckled. "I expect you do, but the city lights probably hide them."

"No doubt you're right. Even in Bygones, the stars don't shine as brightly as they do out here."

"I'd like to see Boston one of these days," he said casually.

She smiled as if remembering all her favorite places. "There's a lot to see."

"Do you miss it?"

She sat up very straight. "Not really, no. I did at first. Everything was so convenient there, and I'll always love certain things about Boston, not to mention my family and friends. But I don't miss it. The city seems terribly busy now. This…this is home."

Tate nodded. It was what he'd hoped, what he'd wanted to hear.

"Can I ask you something?" she asked after a time.

"Anything," he answered, and he meant it.

"Will you be attending church regularly now?"

"Yes," he said without hesitation. "I was foolish to stay away so long."

"Coraline says it was because you were angry with God."

"It was. At first. I just couldn't understand how He could allow Eve to die like that. I still can't."

"But you got over being angry?"

"Yes, I suppose I did. Somewhere along the way, I realized that, though God may have let Eve be taken from me, He had also given me Isabella."

"But you stayed away from church anyway."

"Out of pride, I suppose, and habit. And sheer

idiocy." He sighed and added, "But that's all behind me now. I got it straight between me and God last night. I'm not saying I have everything figured out, but I know where I need to be from now on."

"I'm so glad," Lily told him softly, her eyes glistening behind her glasses.

Tate answered her smile with one of his own. "Say, you know what? I'm going to need some new clothes. That suit I wore this morning felt like it was strangling me."

"Yes, I noticed that it was a bit tight across the shoulders."

"Maybe Isabella and I ought to run into Manhattan tomorrow and do some shopping."

"Or you could go with Kenneth and me on Tuesday," Lily suggested timidly.

"Sure. Or you could go with us and meet Kenneth there," Tate said, smiling. "No reason for Kenneth to tag along on a shopping expedition if he doesn't have to."

"Right," Lily agreed, flashing a wide smile. She ducked her head, and Tate laughed, for no other reason than he felt like it. She laughed, too, and they finished the drive in comfortable silence.

"I'll call Kenneth and explain things to him," Tate told her.

"I'll work it out with Sherie. She doesn't normally close up the shop, but I'm sure she can manage it."

"Maybe we can make a day of it then," Tate said, "since we're going all that way."

He watched her big blue eyes go soft behind the lenses of her glasses. "That sounds wonderful."

"I've been meaning to drive Isabella by my alma mater. This would be a good opportunity to do that. I may not be a lawyer, but I do have a degree in animal husbandry, you know."

She shook her head. "I didn't."

"Now you do. I hope you're suitably impressed."

She laughed. "I am."

"Good."

"Just one thing," she said.

"What's that?"

"Bring your old suit coat with you. Maybe it can be let out."

"Okay. Worth a try."

Meanwhile he'd be praying that he wasn't making a gargantuan mistake, that Lily would ultimately see things his way. Otherwise shopping might be the only future they'd ever have.

Chapter Fourteen

She would not jump to conclusions. All her life Lily had formed crushes on unattainable men, usually from afar. Few had even known of her regard; one or two had. The latter had either chosen to ignore her or—in one particularly humiliating case—to laugh at her, treating her short-lived regard like a cross between his due and a joke. In this case Tate had made it plain that he didn't want to marry again or have more children. Given her history and his, she would be more than merely stupid to get her hopes up.

Besides, if Tate was going to change his mind and marry again, Bygones was filled with more likely candidates than her. Lily ran into them everywhere she went on Monday: tall, curvy Melissa Sweeney with her long red hair and bright green eyes; blue-eyed, brunette Allison True, a local girl returning home to Bygones; Whitney Leigh—Tate liked girls who wore glasses, after all—even Sherie, who smiled so brightly these days that she lit up any room she entered. Tate was bound to have noticed, or soon would, all the young women at church who had cast such admiring glances at him last Sunday.

Oh, Tate had kissed her, true, but when had Lily Farnsworth ever been any man's likeliest prospect?

Still, she looked forward to Tuesday with almost painful anticipation. Lily had dated. Of course, she had dated. She had been asked out to the odd dinner, movie, party, concert…A few times she had even dated the same man repeatedly. Sadly, none of those men had really interested her—or she them. They had each stopped calling; she hadn't minded.

This wasn't even a date, and yet she couldn't have looked forward to it more. She was going to spend a whole day with Tate and Isabella. Beyond that, she dared not contemplate.

She dressed with care, pairing skinny black jeans with a long sleeveless top of cool blue lace. To this she had added skimpy yellow flats and a long wide yellow scarf that could double as a shawl in the evening. She had twisted two long strands of hair at each of her temples and caught them loosely at her nape with a small gold clip. Silver earrings and a number of silver and gold bangles on her right wrist completed her ensemble.

Despite a busy morning Lily couldn't help watching the clock. Even as she discussed and took orders for a wedding anniversary, two birthdays, a college acceptance, a mortgage pay-off and a club luncheon, Lily kept an eye out for Tate. When he finally arrived, however, he took her by surprise, slipping in with Isabella as a customer left, so that she didn't hear the bell herald their arrival.

"You look great."

The sound of his voice made her jump, turn and laugh.

"Thank you."

Isabella beamed at her across the counter, her carroty hair tamed into two thick braids that lay flat against her head. "Daddy says I can buy a new top on account of the hem's coming down on my old one."

"Is that so?" Lily replied, feigning ignorance. She shouldn't be so happy, but she couldn't help it.

"Are you ready to go?"

"I can't leave until Sherie gets here."

"Oh. We'll walk down to the pet store then and exchange a duplicate gift."

Lily checked the clock on the wall. "Won't be long."

Sherie came in less than ten minutes later, and Tate returned with Isabella not long after that. Lily grabbed her handbag, gave last-minute instructions to Sherie and led the way out of the store.

As soon as they reached the truck, Isabella presented her with a piece of paper.

"I almost forgot!"

It was another coloring, this time of a rosebush with pink roses. She had drawn butterflies on it.

"How lovely. Say, I've been meaning to ask you something," Lily remarked as Tate handed her into the front seat of the truck. "After seeing all those childhood mementos on your mother's kitchen walls, I got to wondering where you keep Isabella's."

"I have a special place for them."

Lily waited for him to walk around and get inside. "It's just that my mother had a very organized system. She always displayed our artwork and awards on her desk at work for two weeks. Then it went into a special box. At the end of every year, she sat down with my sister and me to choose two special pieces for each of us to go into a keepsake book. Of course, if it didn't fit in the book, it wasn't saved, but now Mom has a very nice, orderly, year-by-year record of our childhood."

"Oh? That sounds…organized. At least it doesn't take over the whole house that way." Tate started up the truck. "Dad says that there was a time when my sister's and my junk completely took over his and Mom's place. You know how it is, though. Stuff falls apart and gets lost. Only the most tangible things seem to remain. Those don't seem like the kind of things that usually fit into a book."

He eased the truck out into traffic and drove toward Granary Road.

"No," Lily said, "they're not."

"The keepsake book is a good idea, though, for all those colorings and certificates and such. As for the other things, I guess I'll keep hanging them on my bedroom wall."

"So that's where you keep them," Lily said.

"Mmm-hmm. After I cleared out Eve's things, it always looked kind of bare, so when Isabella started presenting me with her artwork, I used it to fill the empty places, and one thing led to another." He shrugged, turning onto Granary and heading south. "Now it's one of my favorite rooms in the house."

"I got almost one whole wall covered," Isabella put in from the backseat. "That leaves three more. I'm saving one in case I get a baby sister someday."

"Isabella!" Tate scolded. "We've talked about that."

"I know, Daddy."

"There aren't going to be any baby sisters."

"But, Da-a-ad."

"I don't want to hear any more about it."

Isabella said nothing more, and neither did Lily. She imagined that they were both equally disappointed by Tate's attitude.

"What do you think?" Tate rolled his shoulders inside the sleek black suit coat.

Lily smoothed her fine hands over his back. "Sleeve length is good. Fits well in the shoulders, but it needs taking in at the waist."

"We can handle that," the salesclerk assured them, producing a thin piece of chalk. A small, dapper man of middle years, he quickly marked up the suit, including the hem on the pants.

"The thing is," Tate told the man as he worked, "we need it done by close of business today. Also, I have another suit coat that needs letting out, if possible." Lily produced the gray jacket and showed the clerk where it needed attention.

The salesclerk checked his wristwatch. "Give us until 9:00 p.m."

"All right."

"Perhaps you'd like to take a look at our dress shirts and silk ties, as well. We have a two-for-one sale going on."

"Won't hurt to look," Tate said, winking at Lily on his way to the dressing room to change back into his jeans. He was actually enjoying this. Lily's eye for color and style had already influenced his choices more than she might realize. She'd passed right over the lighter summer colors and gone straight to the "classics."

"Listen," she'd said, "if you're only going to have one good suit, it has to be a black suit. You can wear a black suit anywhere. Dress it up, dress it down, wear it with a vest, wear it without a vest, tie, no tie, collared shirt, T-shirt, any color, white... Everything else has limitations. With black, your options are unlimited."

She'd apparently forgotten to mention that black looked expensive. That part he'd figured out for himself. When he came out, having handed off the suit to the clerk, she and Isabella had already picked out several shirts and ties for him to look at. The clerk brought over a sports jacket that would work with blue, gray and black. A Western style, it fit nicely without alteration. Tate bought the lot. While the clerk boxed and bagged and scribbled on his sales pad, Lily pulled Tate aside.

"I can't believe you're buying so much. Are you sure about this?"

"Why not?"

"The man who got married in blue jeans and a tuxedo jacket has turned into a clotheshorse?"

"The boy," he corrected gently. "I got married in the same getup that I wore to the senior prom, by the way."

"The prom. Really?"

"It was what all the guys were wearing, not that there's anything wrong with it. I expect I'll be turning up at church in jeans and a sports coat before long. It's just that I'm well past the senior prom now."

"I understand."

"Do you? I married right out of high school. Graduated at the end of May, married the third of August."

"I knew you were young. I didn't realize you were that young."

"I didn't turn eighteen until the following September, and I was just short of twenty when she died."

Lily shook her head. "From prom to marriage in a matter of weeks. I can hardly imagine it."

He smiled, whispering, "I'm trying to imagine what you wore to prom." Turning her to the full-length mirror in the center of the department, he let his gaze roam over her. He'd never seen a woman as well put together as her. Granted, her style wasn't the usual sort. Soft with unexpected twists, unique without being shocking, artistic but entirely approachable, that was Lily, beautiful Lily.

"I didn't go," she said, locking gazes with him in the mirror. "Why would I? None of my friends went. Who wants to stand around in the shadows watching the girls with dates dance?"

He spun her around to face him. "What do you mean, the girls with dates? You mean no one asked you to your prom?"

She looked at him over the rims of her glasses. "To the prom? Tate, no one asked me out in high school, period."

He clapped a hand to the nape of his neck, loudly demanding, "What is wrong with the guys in Boston?" She rolled her eyes, and he couldn't help it. He shook her. Just once. Not very hard. "Don't do that!" he hissed. Of course, by then, everyone in the area was staring at them, including Isabella, who had been sitting on the floor making faces into a mirror for footwear.

He cleared his throat. "Stop selling yourself short."

Lily became very interested in the center of his chest.

"I was awkward," she said softly, "and *stupidly* shy and skinny, so skinny my parents thought I was anorexic. They took me to doctors. It was embarrassing."

"You're not anorexic or stupid."

"I know. I was skinny, and I was painfully shy. As much as I hated it, law school was good for me. You can't get through it without learning to speak in public."

"I'm sure that's so," he told her, "but you're still a better florist than you were a lawyer, and I'm glad because if you weren't, you wouldn't have come to Bygones."

She smiled, and he turned to signal Isabella. "Let's pay and go to the children's department."

He turned toward the checkout counter. "Maybe after we meet Kenneth and have dinner, we can find a movie to kill some time." And he could put his arm around Lily without anyone noticing.

"That could be fun."

And dangerous. This whole thing with Lily was dangerous and foolish. Why, he wondered, couldn't he help himself?

They bought Isabella several new tops, a pair of jeans and a skirt. She declared it Christmas in July. Tate just said that he'd been putting off seeing to their wardrobes for too long. Lily wondered and said nothing, enjoying the whole exercise. They met Kenneth at the bank and completed the transaction concerning the van. Tate invited him to join them for dinner, but Kenneth declined, saying that he had to get back to Bygones and see to his mother and son.

After driving around town to take in the sights, they picked an appropriate movie and sat in a darkened theater, laughing at the 3-D antics of a cast of wisecracking animated animals. Lily was painfully conscious of the arm that Tate draped casually about her shoulders. Neither did the gesture escape Isabella's keen gaze. Even while laughing uproariously, Isabella kept cutting her gaze at Tate's hand, where it rested with such seeming innocence against Lily's upper arm.

Lily couldn't help wondering if Tate had changed his mind about marrying again. He certainly hadn't changed it about having another child, and so far as Lily was concerned, the two went hand in hand. Sitting there next to him, she tried to tell herself that having her own baby wasn't such a big deal, but she couldn't make herself believe it. Why, she asked herself, did the one man who showed a genuine interest in her turn out to be the one man with whom she shouldn't, couldn't, let herself fall in love?

The movie ended, and they walked a yawning Isabella to the truck. Tate belted her into her booster, and it became obvious that she would soon be sleeping, so he left her and Lily sitting out in the park-

ing lot while he rushed into the department store
to pick up his tailoring. Isabella didn't drop off
immediately, however. She lasted long enough to
embarrass Lily thoroughly.

"My dad sure likes you."

Lily licked her lips, glad that Isabella couldn't
see the way her cheeks flamed, and tried to keep
her voice even as she lightly replied, "That's nice."

"He bought ever'thing you picked out today,"
Isabella pointed out, "and he come to church because of your rosebush."

"No. No, now that was because of your birthday
wish," Lily said quickly.

"And he hadn't never taken no other lady to a
movie 'afore," Isabella declared.

Lily swallowed. "Well, that was just because we
had some time to fill, and…"

"My dad sure likes you," Isabella said again,
around a yawn this time.

Lily didn't know what to say next, so she said
nothing at all, and soon, she could tell that Isabella
was sleeping. Tate returned with his well-fitted suit
and a quick, quiet smile.

"She fell asleep, did she?" he whispered.

Lily nodded, and he said no more. Starting up
the truck, he drove them back to Bygones. Along
the way Lily mused over the situation and came to
a satisfactory explanation.

Tate had finally come to the place where he could
let go of Eve and move forward. He had gotten back

into church and begun to make his peace with God. One day perhaps he would be ready to love again. Then he would rethink his position on marriage and children. For now, he was being nice to her, maybe even practicing his flirting a bit. But that's all it was. That's all it could be. Unless...

But no. *Unless* led to castles in the air and foolish dreams. *Unless* had been her downfall too many times in the past. *Unless* would get her heart broken. She wasn't going to do *unless*.

On the other hand, what could it hurt just to ask him what his intentions were? Hadn't she prayed for God to help her be bold and *do* things? If she asked Tate what his feelings for her were now and he got a strange puzzled look on his face or, worse, an amused one, well, she would have her answer. The problem was, she didn't think she could bear that answer. Not again. Not from Tate. All of which meant that it was already too late.

This time, she'd really done it. This time, she'd really fallen in love. And with the wrong man.

Tate guided the truck to the curb. He'd had the whole trip back from Manhattan to think about how to handle this, and he knew just what he wanted to do. First, he smiled at Lily. Then he held a finger to his lips, indicating that they should both be quiet so as not to wake Isabella. Next, he set the interior light switch so that the overhead lamp wouldn't come on when the doors opened. Only then did he kill the engine and pocket the keys before carefully letting himself out of the truck and hurrying around to do the same for Lily. Keeping his hand on her arm, he led her to the apartment door beneath the canopy.

With very deliberate movements he slipped the glasses from Lily's face, folded them and stowed them in his shirt pocket. He cupped her face in his hands, tilted her head, watched her pink lips part slightly, leaned forward and kissed her.

He kissed her until they were both breathless and he'd had all he could stand. Then he just laid his forehead against hers, closed his eyes and let his heart race until it slowed.

Strangely, the boy he had been with Eve seemed to have been better disciplined than the man he now was with Lily. He'd have to do some praying about that. No doubt of it. Straightening, he took her glasses from his pocket and handed them to her. She slipped them on shyly, her hair swinging forward as she bowed her head.

When she looked up again, he saw the questions in her eyes, questions that he knew she would not ask because it wasn't in her nature to do so, questions that he would soon have to ask of her. But not yet.

He wanted a little more time. Maybe, if she loved him…if she loved him *enough,* he would get the answer he needed, and then maybe they could have a future together, her, him and Isabella. Just a little more time…

"Good night, Lily. Thanks for your help today."

"Good night, Tate."

She flashed him a gentle smile and slipped through the door. Grinning, he all but danced around to slide back behind the steering wheel. Just a little more time.

Meanwhile he and Isabella had some work to do at home. She should have a say, after all, in which of her mother's photos remained on display and which were lovingly put away.

Leaning forward, Lily dripped mustard onto the plank table and the paper that had wrapped her hamburger. Tate reached past Isabella and across the table to mop blobs of yellow from Lily's chin.

"I suspect we're all going to look as if we've been shot with a mustard gun before we get to the mid-week service," he muttered.

Thankfully Lily had piled napkins in her lap earlier when it had become obvious that Velma's cuisine was unusually condiment-rich tonight. The Dills were understandably upset by an act of vandalism that had occurred during the wee hours of the morning. Someone had overturned the picnic tables outside and thrown a trash can through a window, stealing several candy bars and a few bags of chips, all items easily reached from outside the store. Elwood had boarded up the broken window and Joe Sheridan had come around to investigate, but a real thief would have taken items of more value. The whole thing was both disturbing and puzzling. Tate couldn't help feeling concerned. The town didn't need this kind of foolishness on top of everything else.

"Why don't you take off your new sport coat?" Lily suggested.

"Good idea," he told her, getting up to stow it in the truck, which sat parked nearby. "Isabella, run inside and get us some more napkins."

Obediently, she rose and went into the grill of The Everything to ask for extra paper napkins. Tate returned to the table to begin dismantling hamburgers and wiping them of their excess mustard.

"Velma must've had a mustard malfunction," Lily said, passing him her burger.

"That's not the only malfunction around here, if you ask me," declared a feminine voice. Tate looked up in time to see Whitney Leigh, the reporter for the *Bygones Gazette,* carrying a stack of newspapers around the front of Tate's truck.

"You come to investigate the break-in?" Tate asked, straightening.

"Why? Do you think it's somehow related to the SOS Committee and the anonymous benefactor?"

"What? Don't tell me you're still beating that drum."

"And I'm going to keep beating it," Whitney insisted. "How can we trust someone who won't reveal his or her identity?"

"Look, all I can tell you is that the town is in the clear."

"That's what you say now, but you haven't read my latest column, have you?"

"No," Tate admitted, "I haven't."

She held out a paper to him, but when he went to take it, she pulled it back again. Tate dug into his pocket for the requisite coins and passed them over. Whitney handed him a copy of the *Gazette,* turned on her heel and carried the remaining stack of papers inside the convenience store. Lily quickly reassembled the hamburgers while Tate came around to her side of the picnic-style table and opened the paper to the editorial column. Isabella returned with clean napkins. Lily wadded up the soiled ones while Tate made sure Isabella was eating before glancing over the column.

Whitney had interviewed a local attorney, Spense O'Laughlin, who lived in Bygones but practiced elsewhere. O'Laughlin had expressed doubt that the city could be liable for any debts incurred should one of the new businesses in town fail, but he had pointed out that they were dealing with several unknowns, not the least of which was the identity of the "entity" funding the grants.

"Do you know this O'Laughlin?" Lily asked Tate.

"I do. He voiced similar concerns to the SOS Committee when we consulted with him while drawing up the conditions for the matching grants, but we were as helpless to do anything about the situation then as we are now."

"Very convenient, if you ask me," Whitney said, returning without the burden of newspapers. Presumably she'd left them at the counter inside to be sold. "How is it that this benefactor is available to give business advice but can still hide his or her identity?"

"You already know that," Tate retorted. "Everything is done by email."

"Has anyone even tried to track that?"

"Presumably the committee signed an agreement with the benefactor agreeing not to do any such thing," Lily said.

"That's right," Tate told her with a smile. His secret attorney knew a thing or two, after all.

"Well, I didn't sign any such agreement!" Whitney declared.

"I don't see what difference it really makes," Lily said. "I think it's all quite admirable. Whoever the benefactor is, he or she has done a generous thing, a good thing."

"You would think so," Tate told her, smiling. "You're too sweet to assign ulterior motives."

"What ulterior motives could there be?"

Tate shrugged. "I don't know. I just think it's suspicious that it's kept a secret."

Lily linked her arm with his. "Maybe you're the mysterious benefactor and you're just saying that to throw us off the scent."

He smiled. "Sorry, sweetheart. I don't have that kind of money, and I'm not that generous. Frankly, such a scheme would never have occurred to me. And if it had, I can't think why I'd want to make a secret of my identity. Uh-uh. Not this guy."

Thankfully Lily didn't seem disappointed.

"It has to be someone around here," Whitney said, "and I'm going to find out who it is if it's the last thing I do." With that, she turned and stalked away, her hands tight little fists swinging at her sides.

"Whoever it is," Lily said, "I expect he or she has met his or her match. That is one determined woman."

"I expect you are right," Tate agreed.

Just then Nancy Jacobs called to Isabella, asking if she'd like to help Bonnie watch her baby sister while she, Nancy, closed up the Snow Cone Cabin.

"Can I, Daddy?"

As she'd managed to eat over half of her hamburger, he let her go.

"We'd better eat our own burgers," Lily said, reaching for hers.

Tate nodded, following suit. "You don't think Pastor Garman will faint when he sees me walk into the church for the second time in the same week, do you?"

Her mouth full, Lily elbowed him then tried to eat while laughing.

Quickly finishing the meal, Tate gathered up the

refuse and carried it to the trash barrel once more positioned beside the door. Elwood had weighted it with chains threaded through concrete blocks. Lily stood and brushed crumbs from her skirt. Isabella ran over to Lily, carrying Bonnie's baby sister on her hip. The plump baby giggled, her fists wrapped in Isabella's bright hair. Bonnie ran alongside, trying to free Isabella's hair from her sister's greedy gasp.

"Isn't she cute?" Isabella gushed.

"She's adorable," Lily said, taking the baby into her arms so Bonnie could more easily disentangle her little hands.

"Let go," Bonnie scolded mildly, finally succeeding in freeing Isabella's hair.

"Wouldn't it be fun to have a baby?" Isabella said.

"Oh, yes!" Lily agreed.

Tate froze in midstride.

"I love babies," Lily went on brightly, juggling the baby higher in her arms. The baby reached for Lily's glasses, but she neatly avoided her tiny grasp, laughing. "Oh, no, you don't. I know all the baby tricks, and you can't have my glasses, little miss." She smacked loud kisses on the giggling baby's cheek, while Tate stood frozen in place.

Seeing her now, he knew he'd been fooling himself, pretending that Lily could be content with him and Isabella. If he married Lily, of course she would want to have a baby of her own. For an instant Tate pictured Lily big with his child, her slender frame swollen with pregnancy. She would be as graceful and achingly beautiful as ever, her sweet smile hopeful and loving. His heart swelled with pride. Then fear shuddered through him, fear unlike anything he'd ever known.

If Lily had a baby, she could die, and he could not face the possibility of such loss again. Yet how could he ask Lily to give up the possibility of a child of her own?

Could he be that selfish? Even if it was the only way that they could be together? For it was, he realized with a leaden heart, the *only* way they could be together.

Chapter Fifteen

❧

"Night and day," Lily said, twisting her hands together. "That's the only way I know how to describe it. We were talking about the mystery benefactor who funded the grants and brought the new businesses to town. I laughingly suggested that it might be Tate, and he flatly denied it. I believed him. Then Isabella brought over Bonnie's baby sister, but it was almost time for church, so we had to go, and that's when everything changed."

Coraline shook her head, looking like the prim school principal that she was, sitting there on Lily's unconventional couch. "He did seem very distracted during the Wednesday service."

"He didn't sing along with any of the hymns," Lily revealed softly, "and he didn't speak a word to me on the way home."

"And you haven't heard from him since?"

"Not in two days, and I've left three messages on his phone."

"I see."

"The thing is," Lily went on, hardly able to meet Coraline's gaze, "I have a history of, well, forming attachments to unattainable men. It usually doesn't get this far. That is, it's usually all…me. This time, though, I thought…" She shook her head. Perhaps she had misread his intentions, after all. Those kisses probably hadn't meant a thing. Still, Tate didn't seem like the sort to lead a girl on. "I—I don't know what to do or say now. I've never been in this position before. Should I apologize, back off? What?"

Coraline smiled. "I don't see that you have anything to apologize for, Lily. I think we should just pray about this matter and see what happens."

Somewhat comforted, Lily nodded. "Thank you. I'd like that." She bowed her head. Coraline began to speak. After the prayer, Coraline rose to leave.

"Now, don't you worry about a thing," Coraline said. "God will work it out."

Lily thanked her for coming, certain that she was right. God would take care of everything. Whatever happened, she had found good friends here in Bygones. That counted for a lot. It might even, eventually, make up for a broken heart, but maybe it wouldn't come to that. Every relationship must have its ups and downs. She could be making a mountain out of a molehill here. Tate could walk into the shop tomorrow or the next day and they might carry on as if nothing had ever happened.

Lily felt a certain peace after that. She was glad that she'd called Coraline. She only wished that she'd called earlier instead of moping around about it for two days. It was true that Tate had been distracted during the service on Wednesday. He'd sat with his head down the whole time; Lily had told herself that he was concentrating on the short message and prayer requests, but then he'd sent Isabella home with his parents. Withdrawn, distant, he hadn't spoken a word on the drive back to her place, and when they'd arrived, he hadn't gotten out or come around to open her door. He'd only nodded when she'd told him good-night, and he hadn't even waited for her to get inside before he'd driven away that night.

After a day of silence, she'd left a message on his cell phone, but he hadn't called back. The next morning, she'd asked, via phone message, if she had offended him in some way. The silence since had been deafening. Finally, in desperation, she'd called Coraline to ask her advice.

Lily didn't expect Coraline to talk to Tate, but when she heard a knock on her door late that night and opened it to find a shamefaced Tate standing there, Lily knew that's what had happened.

"Oh, no. Coraline came to see you, didn't she?"

"She was right to," he said, sliding past Lily and

down the narrow entry into the living area. He needed a shave, and the jeans and T-shirt that he wore looked rumpled.

"Is everything all right?" Lily asked, sensing his tension. "Is Isabella—"

"Isabella's with my mom," he said, "but no, everything isn't 'all right.' Lily, I have to ask you something. I should have asked it as soon as I realized how I feel about you."

Lily's heart leaped. "Tate? What do you mean, how you feel about me?"

He gusted a sigh and rubbed both hands over his face. "Lily, I like you." He threw out his hands. "Who am I kidding? I'm crazy about you! I haven't ever been so wrapped up in a woman, but…" He shook his head. "I know you love Isabella."

"Of course I do."

He tilted his head. "But is that enough?"

"Enough?"

"What I mean is, would you want…would you need to have your own child, your own baby?"

There could be only one answer to that, but she stalled a bit, hoping against hope. "Naturally I would *want* my own child. As for *needing* my own child, I don't know if I'd put it that way exactly, but…" She tried to think of another way to say it, a way to make it acceptable somehow. In the end it could be said only one way. "Yes, I would expect to have a baby." Or two.

He closed his eyes. "I can't," he stated flatly.

Lily gulped. "When you say you can't, do you mean—"

He looked her straight in the eye and said, "I won't."

She knew she hadn't misheard that. "You're saying that you *refuse* to have another child."

"That's right. I refuse. Period."

For a long moment Lily said and did nothing, until finally the full implications of that settled over her. "I see." She felt amazingly calm, considering that the very last spark of hope had just died within her. "I could say that is a deal breaker, but we don't really have a deal, do we?"

Tate bowed his head. "No, we don't."

"Well," she said, reeling emotionally, "thank you for being honest with me."

"Lily, I'm sorry. I thought we might... I really hoped..."

"Could you go now?" she asked evenly, feeling very brittle.

Nodding, he moved toward the entry, only to stop, but then he merely glanced back, nodded and left.

Lily stood where she was for a moment. Then she walked over to the dining table and sank onto one of the stools there. After a moment she folded her arms, laid her head down and sobbed.

She should have known. She should have known. On some level, she had. All those kisses aside, she had never really believed that Tate could feel for her what she felt for him. Things like that didn't happen to women like her. She told herself that she would survive this, just as she had survived other disappointments. But, oh, how this hurt, worse than anything before, worse than anything she had imagined.

Always before, it had been pie in the sky, castles in the air, one-sided and imaginary. This time…this time, she'd almost gotten it right. Almost. Funny, but almost was worse than anything else had ever been. She wished to be that woman again, the one whom the guy simply did not notice. It was easier that way. Safer.

Lily indulged herself in the pain all that night and all day on Saturday, staying in and letting Sherie handle the shop alone. Sherie was completely frazzled when she came up at the end of the day to check on Lily. Seeing Lily's red eyes and nose, Sherie assumed that Lily had a cold and offered to make her a pot of mint tea, saying that she needed the boss "in fighting shape by Monday," which was Sherie's scheduled day off.

"Don't worry, you'll have Monday off, as planned." A busy mom, Sherie needed Sunday and Monday with her boys.

"Okay. You're the boss."

Lily remembered that the next day, Sunday, when she spoke to Coraline after church. Tate had not shown up, and Lily felt sure that he wouldn't as long as she was there. She didn't have to stay. Yes, if she gave up the shop, she'd be buried in debt, but she could always go back to practicing law, and if she did, her parents and grandparents would likely help her.

"Maybe I should just go home to Boston."

"Lily, you have obligations here," Coraline reminded her. "People are depending on you. Sherie, to name only one. To be quite frank, the town is depending on you."

"I know, but…"

Coraline hugged her. "Just think about it, dear. I'm praying for you."

Lily nodded.

Back at the apartment she wandered around for an hour or so. Then she remembered something that she'd seen on the computer one day weeks ago. She went downstairs and searched through her email in-box until she found a certain notice that she'd glanced at and dismissed. Closing her eyes, she bowed her head and said a quick prayer, then she sent off an email and received an immediate response. Encouraged, she reached for her phone.

"Coraline, I need a ride to the airport."

To her surprise, Coraline promptly agreed. Things fell into place quickly. Giving herself no time for second-guessing, Lily called Sherie, apologized for the short notice, explained herself, then ran upstairs to pack.

Bygones had become her home, and she had friends here, good friends, dear friends, but that didn't mean she couldn't, shouldn't, leave. She cared about what happened to this town. She loved her little shop, but she had to think of herself, too. She had to find a way to heal her heart, a way to go on. God would work it all out. Somehow.

He didn't mean to drive down Main Street. That wasn't part of the plan at all. But somehow Tate turned a block too soon. Instead of turning off Granary Road onto Municipal Place and then into the post office parking lot, Tate found himself in the middle of Main Street. Then, of course, he just happened to glance across the way as he passed Love in Bloom, and that was when he threw on the brakes.

The sign in the window said, in big block letters, "Closed Until Further Notice."

His heart stopped. He yanked the truck to the curb and hit the pavement running, nearly knocking his hat off and dodging another pedestrian and a passing sedan on his way across the street. The door to the shop was, as expected, locked, and all the lights inside were off. He ran to the apartment door, through it and up the stairs. The door on the landing at the top refused to budge, but Lily didn't answer his knock, no matter how hard he pounded.

Tate got out his cell phone and dialed her number. The call went straight to voice mail. He didn't leave a message. What was he going to say? *Where are you? Have I driven you away? You can't leave!* He had no right to demand her whereabouts; he probably *had* driven her away, and she certainly could leave anytime she wished.

Starting back down the stairs, he stumbled and nearly fell. Alarmed, he sank onto the nearest step and covered his face with his hands.

What if she had truly left? What if he never saw her again?

Sudden tears clogged his nose and filled his eyes. Wildly, he told himself that she was gone, not dead, but a cold voice inside his head declared that if he never saw her again, she might as well be dead, so far as his heart was concerned. Bleakly he faced the hard truth of that. Without Lily, his life would forever be lived in shades of gray, all the bright, glowing colors leached away by numbness and emptiness, all for shallow safety.

"Oh, dear God, what have I done?" he asked, clasping his hands together and tilting his head back so far that the brim of his rigid straw cowboy hat touched his collar.

He'd thought that if she loved him enough, she wouldn't need a child of her own. He hadn't stopped to think that if he loved her enough, he'd take any risk to have her for however long the good Lord saw fit to let them be together.

"Lord, I'm a fool. I can't live my life without this woman now, not so long as she's in this world. I'm so scared You'll take her away from me that I've thrown her away! And after You brought her straight to me. I don't know what to do except try to find her and...*deserve* her and...make it all right somehow, but You'll have to help me. Please, help me."

After a few moments he got up and went out to visit the bakery and bookstore, but neither Melissa Sweeney nor Allison True had spoken to Lily since Friday, though both had seen her at church on Sunday. He, of course, had stayed away, unable to face her, unable to see her, even at a distance. What a rotten coward he was! He hadn't even gone to face her with the truth of his fears until Coraline had forced the issue, but he had only *thought* he was afraid of losing her before this. Now he was terrified that he had done so.

Tate crossed the street to speak to Miss Mars, who rather coolly advised him to speak to Coraline. He'd hoped to avoid that, but he should've saved himself the time and gone to her straightaway. Miss Mars felt that Coraline could be found in her office at the school, so rather than call, Tate got back in the truck and drove over there.

He felt quite chastened going in—and more so going out again, but he left armed with an address, prayer and at least a shred of hope.

Kicking off her shoes, Lily padded to the bed and collapsed. It had been a long, busy day, but she'd made good contacts and gotten great ideas for the future. Someone knocked on the door, the thuds reverberating off the heavy metal with head-jarring intensity. Why did hotels use metal doors, anyway? Wood was so much nicer and quieter. Groaning, she hauled herself up and went to tell the nuisance that a mistake had been made. She hadn't ordered room service, sent out any dry cleaning or asked for extra towels, and she didn't know a soul in Chicago.

"You have the wrong room," she called through the door, not even bothering to look through the peephole.

"Lily, let me in."

The voice, though muffled, was clearly recognizable, but what was *Tate* doing in Chicago? Astonished, Lily could do nothing for a moment but stare at her own reflection in the mirrored door of the closet.

"Lily, please. I've been waiting downstairs for hours."

Shaken out of her shock, Lily smoothed the line of her skirt. She realized that she was wearing exactly what she'd worn the first day they'd met, her blue dress with white leggings beneath it. The light blue fabric had just enough elasticity to resist wrinkles and add flow to the short wide sleeves and long skirt. The leggings offered support for a long day of travel or, in this case, walking, and removed the necessity of a slip, plus they made the ballet flats work. She wished she didn't look so tired, but she could do nothing about that now.

Gathering her long hair, she twisted it into a rope, pulled it over one shoulder and opened the door.

Tate stood there in his jeans and sport coat, one of his new shirts open at the collar. He held his hat in his hands, head bowed meekly. Her heart started to pound at the sight of him.

"Can I come in?"

"Yes, of course."

He walked past her into the room and tossed his hat onto the little round dining table in the corner at the foot of the bed. Then he turned, threw out his arms and demanded, "What are you doing in Chicago?"

Lily parked her hands on her hips. She owed him no explanations. He wasn't her boss. She was the boss at Love in Bloom. He was nothing more than her official contact with the SOS Committee, and so long as she didn't break her contract with them, he had no say in where she went or what she did. Still, Lily being Lily, she gave him an answer.

"I'm attending a flower show, obviously."

He mimicked her stance. "Don't you think you should've let me know where you were going?"

Lily folded her arms. "I don't see why."

"Because I need to know," he exclaimed. "In fact, I need to know where you are every minute of every day. Not knowing makes me nuts! I can't live without knowing." He shoved a hand through his hair, adding, "I can't live without *you*."

Lily dropped her arms, frowning. She'd heard what he'd said, but somehow the words didn't compute. "I—I'm not sure what you're saying."

"Yes, you are," he grumbled. Then he straightened and looked her in the eye. "I'm saying that I love you."

"Tate!" Lily gasped.

"Despite my better judgment," he went on doggedly, "despite my fears, despite my pigheadedness..." He held out both hands to her. "I love you, Lily. I can't help it. I love you so much it scares me, and I'm sorry for being such a fool."

"Tate!"

"I didn't want to fall in love again, but you're so sweet and generous and kind. I can't imagine my life without you anymore."

"Oh, Tate, I love you, too!"

She flew at him. He reached for her, but just before his hands closed on her waist, she stopped, drawing up onto her tiptoes. She had to know exactly where they stood, exactly what she was in for, not that she could go back now, whatever he said next.

"Does this mean you'll consider having another child? If you'll just say that you'll think about it, we can—"

"I'll think about it," he said firmly.

She pressed her hands together and brought her fingertips to rest beneath her chin in an expression of gratitude. "Thank you. I know how difficult this is for you."

"Who am I kidding?" he asked in an exasperated tone. "I'll do more than think about it," he said.

"It'll terrify me, but, sweetheart, I'll do anything that makes you and Isabella happy."

"Oh, Tate."

"I'm willing to risk anything for you. For us. If you'll just come back home to Bygones and marry me."

Lily let herself fall into him, throwing her arms around his neck.

"Yes!" she cried. "Oh, yes!"

"We'll have babies, if that's what you want."

"Babies." She relished the plurality.

"I've been praying about it nonstop," he told her, hugging her close, "and I'll keep praying about it for however long God gives us."

"That," Lily promised, smiling and crying all at once, "is going to be a long, long time."

Coraline had been right. God had worked it all out. Perfectly.

Biting into a strawberry cake so sweet that it made her teeth ache, Lily moaned with delight. "Oh, Melissa. This is scrumptious."

Melissa Sweeney, baker extraordinaire, had brought several small cakes from the bakery next door to the flower shop, so Lily could begin to narrow down her choices for a wedding cake. She and Tate had set a date for the first Friday in October. That gave them just over two months to pull off a wedding that her Boston family, while thrilled, clearly expected to be an embarrassment. Lily knew it was going to be perfect. She, Tate and Isabella were flying to Boston in a week to introduce her future husband and daughter to her family and shop for dresses.

"What's scrumptious is that ring," Melissa said, catching Lily's hand to admire the diamond sparkling on her ring finger.

"Isn't it something? Tate bought it in Chicago."

"That man is over the moon for you."

"Can you believe it?" Lily asked, scrunching her shoulders.

"It's clearly mutual," Melissa said with a smile.

"Oh, it is," Lily admitted dreamily.

Melissa chuckled. "I should've been so fortunate with my SOS Committee contact."

"Who is your contact?"

"Dale Eversleigh."

Lily dropped her gaze and used a small pink paper napkin to delicately wipe her lips. "Oh."

Melissa grinned. "Dale is a nice guy."

"Very nice."

"In a loud-plaid or solemn-undertaker sort of way."

Lily couldn't contain her smile, remembering the day that Tate had insisted that the stout, bewigged mortician had been "hitting on" her. She loved the idea that Tate had been just a teensy bit jealous.

"Especially if you like golf."

They both giggled, then Melissa said, "Well, I don't have time for golf—or much of anything else right now. I've got to hire some full-time help. The thing is, though, Dale Eversleigh's take on the individuals on my list of prospective employees is that one is as good as another. Do you think Tate might have a better perspective?"

"He might," Lily said. "Who's on the list?"

Melissa reached into her apron pocket and brought out a folded sheet of paper. Lily put aside her cake for the moment in order to go over the list with the baker.

"I know a few of these people," she said, "but Tate will know them far better, of course." She pulled over a pad and jotted down the names. When she came to one in particular, she struck a line through it. "I can't imagine how Brian Montclair's name got on here," she said, "but trust me, you don't want to hire him."

"What makes you say that?"

"At the reception following the Grand Opening," Lily told her, "Brian was quite critical of my 'fancy flowers' and your 'girly cakes.' He called my flower arrangements 'nuts' and said that our grants were a waste of funds. Tate said he was just mad because the committee didn't choose a mechanic's shop to receive one of the grants, and I can certainly understand that, but I thought Brian was unnecessarily disagreeable about the whole thing, frankly."

"I can't imagine that he wants to work for me, then," Melissa said, folding the list and tucking it away again. "Someone must have made a mistake when they put his name on my list."

"That would be my guess," Lily told her.

"Will you let me know if Tate has any insights for me about the others on the list?"

"Right away."

"Great. Now, there's one other little question on my mind before we get back to choosing the flavor of your wedding cake."

"What's that?"

"Josh Smith has suggested that we newcomers ought to get together, say, once a month, maybe, just to check in with each other, see how things are going with our businesses. There's even talk of including the SOS Committee. What do you think?"

"Works for me," Lily said with a decisive nod. "Yes, I like it. Why not?"

"He's offering the Cozy Cup Café after hours as a meeting place."

"Sounds good."

"Great. I'll let everyone else know you're on board. You'll speak to Tate about it?"

"Sure."

"Cool."

"Back to the fun stuff." Lily pulled the cake plate forward, turned it, picked up a sweet little bundle of yellow-and-cream goodness and bit into the most divine pineapple cake. "Oooh. You're making this decision wonderfully difficult, aren't you?"

Melissa smiled. "Take your time. You can let me know your decision later."

Lily licked her fingers and reached for a beautiful miniature cake the color of a frosted pumpkin.

"Talk to you later," Melissa said, waving as she headed out the door of the flower shop.

Lily smiled, pausing a moment to admire the ridiculously large diamond on her finger. Sighing happily, she bit into the most mouthwatering bit of orange cake she'd ever tasted.

Before she could even swallow, the bell over the door jingled, and the most wonderful man in the world ushered the most precious little girl into the shop.

"Hi, Lily!" Isabella all but sang.

With her mouth full, Lily could only wave. She gulped down the cake as Tate slipped past his smiling daughter to lean over the counter and kiss Lily.

"Mmm, sweet," he said, lifting his head.

Lily chuckled. "If you think that's sweet, you should taste this." She shoved a tiny white square decorated with green into his mouth.

"Mint," he murmured, chewing, but as soon as he swallowed, he kissed her again. "Nope. You're sweeter."

Isabella snorted. "Oh, brother."

He shook a finger at her. "Hey, watch it. You're the one who wanted me to fall in love and get married again."

"Yeah, so I could have a mom and a baby sister,"

she said, trying not to grin, "but I didn't know you were gonna get all mushy."

"Well, get used to it," he told her, winking at Lily. "I'm officially mush."

Lily laughed. "I love the two of you."

Isabella ran around the counter and threw her arms around Lily. "We love you, too. Can I have some cake?"

"Of course."

She lifted the girl up onto the counter and let her choose her own sample.

Who would have dreamed just a month ago, that she'd be choosing wedding cake today? She'd just agreed to a monthly newcomers' meeting, but she no longer felt like a newcomer. Bygones was her home, and she would not believe that God had brought her here only to let this wonderful little town die.

No one could ever tell what God would do, of course, but everyone could always trust that it would be for the best. She was living proof of that.

Looking back now, she saw that going to law school had been one of the best things to happen to her. Even if she hoped never to practice law, being forced to endure law school had gone a long way to helping her overcome her shyness. Without that, she'd never have had the courage to apply for the grant that had brought her here to Bygones. She'd never have opened her shop, never have met Tate and Isabella, never have found this love and known this happiness.

Together they would build a good life and fight for this town that they all loved. This was where she and Tate would raise their family. Of course, they didn't have to start adding to the family right away. They had lots of time.

Meanwhile she knew they could save the town, all working together, the Committee, the new business owners, the townsfolk. So long as they kept depending on God and each other, they could rescue this lovely place and its sweet way of life. The future might seem a bit uncertain still, but from where Lily stood, it looked bright.

She took Tate's hand with her right and slipped her left one over Isabella's bright curls, the diamond in her engagement ring sparkling in the light.

Yes, the future looked very bright, indeed.

* * * * *

Dear Reader,

Not long ago, my husband and I made a big move from the DFW Metroplex in Texas, where we lived for 33 years, to the scenic Ozarks of northwest Arkansas. Happily, I have experience on the other end of the spectrum, too, as I was blessed to grow up in the small town of Comanche, Oklahoma.

Big cities have much to recommend them: so much to see and do, so many conveniences! But nothing can replace the community spirit of small-town life. I firmly believe that people are people the world over, but small-town folk always have time for one another. They turn out for every occasion, and they're quick to spread hugs and laughter.

Lily hoped to find that sense of community in Bygones, and I think she did. I hope you experienced it through her eyes and that you'll visit again and again.

God bless,

Arlene James

Questions for Discussion

1. Today, many communities find themselves in the position of Bygones, Kansas. What do you think of the solution with which Bygones was presented?

2. Lily made a big transition, moving from the large cosmopolitan area of Boston to a small town in Kansas. How difficult do you suppose such a transition would be in real life? Why?

3. Coraline Connolly is a woman of unusual faith and wisdom. A widow, dedicated to her calling as an educator, she possesses an uncommon insight into human behavior. Have you ever known a real person with such attributes? If so, who, and how did that person impact your life?

4. Shyness can be a great handicap. The extroverts among us may not understand how shyness affects interaction. Are you shy? Can you help others understand?

5. Lily was inspired by items that she found in Miss Mars's junk room behind the This 'N' That. To some, junk is just junk. To the creative, however, it may be a work of art. What inspires you?

6. After losing Eve so tragically, Tate tried hard not to be attracted to Lily or any woman, but his upbringing worked against him. He couldn't leave a newcomer alone on a holiday, after all. Why did his blunt explanation about Eve and his decision never to marry again fail to protect him from involvement with Lily? Why does talking about our feelings open us to involvement?

7. The Grand Opening was a great success; so why were so many of the townsfolk skeptical of the plan to save the city? Why are we so often afraid to hope?

8. Tate's attraction to Lily grew when he recognized her great creativity. Why is creativity an attractive quality?

9. Tate felt that Lily should hire Kenneth Wilbur to work in her shop because Kenneth's need was greater than that of Sherie, whom Lily did hire. Do you think Tate was right? Why or why not?

10. Lily was heartbroken to learn that Tate had refused to attend church out of anger at God after the death of his beloved wife. Have you ever been angry at God? What did you do about it?

11. Anger and fear often walk hand in hand; yet even after Tate's anger over his wife's death had

softened, his fear of suffering a similar loss remained and even grew after he came to care for Lily. How does one conquer fear?

12. The Wilburs were in great financial distress. The community garden helped them and others, and it also helped bring the town together for a common cause. Why is that important in times of social and financial stress? Is your community experiencing such stress? Have you taken steps to bring your community together? If so, what were they?

13. Tate finally found the strength to let go of his late wife's memory after his daughter pointed out how happy her mom must be in Heaven, and he found the strength to return to church after Isabella made a birthday "wish" or prayer for him to do so. Has someone else ever given you the impetus or strength to do what you knew you should?

14. Lily had come to Bygones to get away from what she saw as the failures of her past. She'd allowed herself to be coerced into training for an occupation for which she had zero affinity. She'd never had a serious boyfriend but had instead built imaginary relationships with men who didn't even know she existed. She'd struggled with envy toward her more outgoing and

accomplished sister. Nevertheless, she stayed true to herself and hung on to her faith, and God rewarded her for that with true love. Does that seem right and reasonable to you? Why or why not?

15. Tate feared losing Lily in the same way that he'd lost Eve, only to realize that he'd lost Lily by driving her away with his unreasonable fear. He concluded that the only way to have Lily was to let go of his fear. What might you have if you could let go of your fear?

LARGER-PRINT BOOKS!

GET 2 FREE
LARGER-PRINT NOVELS
PLUS 2 FREE
MYSTERY GIFTS

Love Inspired

Larger-print novels are now available...

LILPDIR13R

LARGER-PRINT BOOKS!

GET 2 FREE LARGER-PRINT NOVELS PLUS 2 FREE MYSTERY GIFTS

Love Inspired
SUSPENSE
RIVETING INSPIRATIONAL ROMANCE

Larger-print novels are now available...

YES! Please send me 2 FREE LARGER-PRINT Love Inspired® Suspense novels and my 2 FREE mystery gifts (gifts are worth about $10). After receiving them, if I don't wish to receive any more books, I can return the shipping statement marked "cancel." If I don't cancel, I will receive 4 brand-new novels every month and be billed just $5.24 per book in the U.S. or $5.74 per book in Canada. That's a savings of at least 23% off the cover price. It's quite a bargain! Shipping and handling is just 50¢ per book in the U.S. and 75¢ per book in Canada.* I understand that accepting the 2 free books and gifts places me under no obligation to buy anything. I can always return a shipment and cancel at any time. Even if I never buy another book, the two free books and gifts are mine to keep forever.

110/310 IDN F5CC

Name	(PLEASE PRINT)	
Address		Apt. #
City	State/Prov.	Zip/Postal Code

Signature (if under 18, a parent or guardian must sign)

Mail to the Harlequin® Reader Service:
IN U.S.A.: P.O. Box 1867, Buffalo, NY 14240-1867
IN CANADA: P.O. Box 609, Fort Erie, Ontario L2A 5X3

Are you a current subscriber to Love Inspired Suspense books and want to receive the larger-print edition?
Call 1-800-873-8635 or visit www.ReaderService.com.

LISLPDIR13R

REQUEST YOUR FREE BOOKS!
2 FREE WHOLESOME ROMANCE NOVELS IN LARGER PRINT
PLUS 2 FREE MYSTERY GIFTS

✿✿✿✿✿✿✿✿✿✿✿✿✿✿✿✿✿✿✿

HEARTWARMING™

Wholesome, tender romances

YES! Please send me 2 FREE Harlequin® Heartwarming Larger-Print novels and my 2 FREE mystery gifts (gifts worth about $10). After receiving them, if I don't wish to receive any more books, I can return the shipping statement marked "cancel." If I don't cancel, I will receive 4 brand-new larger-print novels every month and be billed just $4.99 per book in the U.S. or $5.74 per book in Canada. That's a savings of at least 23% off the cover price. It's quite a bargain! Shipping and handling is just 50¢ per book in the U.S. and 75¢ per book in Canada.* I understand that accepting the 2 free books and gifts places me under no obligation to buy anything. I can always return a shipment and cancel at any time. Even if I never buy another book, the two free books and gifts are mine to keep forever.

161/361 IDN F47N

Name   (PLEASE PRINT)

Address   Apt. #

City   State/Prov.   Zip/Postal Code

Signature (if under 18, a parent or guardian must sign)

Mail to the Harlequin® Reader Service:
IN U.S.A.: P.O. Box 1867, Buffalo, NY 14240-1867
IN CANADA: P.O. Box 609, Fort Erie, Ontario L2A 5X3

* Terms and prices subject to change without notice. Prices do not include applicable taxes. Sales tax applicable in N.Y. Canadian residents will be charged applicable taxes. Offer not valid in Quebec. This offer is limited to one order per household. Not valid for current subscribers to Harlequin Heartwarming larger-print books. All orders subject to credit approval. Credit or debit balances in a customer's account(s) may be offset by any other outstanding balance owed by or to the customer. Please allow 4 to 6 weeks for delivery. Offer available while quantities last.

Your Privacy—The Harlequin® Reader Service is committed to protecting your privacy. Our Privacy Policy is available online at www.ReaderService.com or upon request from the Harlequin Reader Service.

We make a portion of our mailing list available to reputable third parties that offer products we believe may interest you. If you prefer that we not exchange your name with third parties, or if you wish to clarify or modify your communication preferences, please visit us at www.ReaderService.com/consumerschoice or write to us at Harlequin Reader Service Preference Service, P.O. Box 9062, Buffalo, NY 14269. Include your complete name and address.

HWDIR13R